LISA MANIFOLD

FOREVER BLOOD

VAMPIRE BRIDES

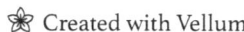

"Every man's heart one day beats its final beat. His lungs breathe a final breath. And if what that man did in his life makes the blood pulse through the body of others and makes them bleed deeper and something larger than life, then his essence, his spirit, will be immortalized."

James Hellwig

THE VAMPIRES OF CLAN MACLEAN

Lochdon House
Isle of Mull, Scotland

Angus–Kyla's mate
Charlotte–Talbot's mate
Clara–Lyall's mate
Collum -not mated
Devon–Margaret's mate
Kyla–Angus' mate
Lyall–Clara's mate
Margaret–Devon's mate
Morag–not mated
Talbot–Charlotte's mate

PROLOGUE

Collum
1483
Sound of Mull, Scotland

There were worse ways to die, I supposed. At least if I died today, it would be with honor. If only it wasn't so damned cold. That was more annoying than the thought of dying in battle. No honor in freezing your bollocks off. I shivered as I looked over the rail of the galley. The wind whipped through the ranks of men who stood around me, making the lines along the mast hum next to the wood. The sails billowed at each gust. The men, myself included, huddled together. There was enough wind that the rowers were all below, their oars stowed so as to not fly about and cause greater damage than the wind was already inflicting.

I looked to my father, William MacLean. We were here because of our allegiance and alliance with the Clan MacLeod, and while John MacDonald, the Lord of the Isles, was greatly diminished in power due to his negotiations with Edward IV of

England, his word and wishes still carried great weight The Scottish king, James III, only in power a few years, had proved to be an evil, lawless man. My father supported John MacDonald, and like a good son and a member of our clan, I followed my father.

In truth, I wasn't so sure. James was the king, albeit a rotten one. If we rose against a king we did not like, and respect, when would we ever have one?

My musings over history came to an end as the boat heaved to port.

"God damn Angus Og!" the captain screamed into the wind.

Angus Og, the son of John MacDonald I stood for, felt his father was no longer fit to lead the clan. This meeting on the Sound of Mull would settle that question once and for all. Well, in the eyes of the law. The Isle of Mull would be divided over this for generations. Scots have long memories and are not at all forgiving.

"What is going on?" I asked my father.

He leaned over, not taking his eyes off the captain, and the crew now scurrying to do God knew what with the lines and sails. "We're goin' ashore. The galley is taking on water, and the captain doesn't want to risk it."

"How did I miss all that?" I wondered.

Now my father turned to look at me, his mouth tipped up in a half-smile. "You were awa' with the fairies, I expect. This might not be the best time for such, Collum," he added.

I laughed, causing the men around me to look at me with suspicion. "Perhaps not, Father. I take heed of your warning."

"See that you do. This conflict is already tearing us apart. No doubt today will all but finish the job."

Everyone jerked forward as the galley ran ashore.

"Get off! Everyone off! Crew only," bellowed the captain. "I'm not sinkin' because of ya, no matter what the Lord of the Isles has to say."

"Careful," my father muttered.

We joined the rest of the men in jumping into the water, which was cold and nearly froze my knees the moment I landed in it. No lass in sight to help me warm the parts of me that needed it more than my knees, either. I ignored it and pushed forward to the shore. Then we turned and waited.

Angus Og's galleys could see us. They would know that we'd only put ashore because something had gone amiss.

We were vulnerable.

Dark was but an hour away and still we waited. The Og's galleys had come closer, but none showed the intention to fight. My father joined some of the men who were taking it in turn to gaze out onto the sound with a spyglass, to keep watch. We'd lit no fires, not wanting to offer the other side a beacon. The men hunkered down in their plaids, crouched low for warmth.

I turned, gazing on the headland behind the beach. Something—the wind—moved along top of it. But I saw nothing.

And then in a moment they were upon us. Swords and axes flashing in the fading sunlight, their screams of war rolling down the beach like a long wave.

I whirled to intercept the sword aimed for my skull. The clang of the two swords meeting rang out over me, and I felt the impact shudder down my arm.

He was a large lad, burly and muscled. A smith, perhaps. He swung the sword with skill, although he was not fast. But he was strong, stronger than me.

And he was pushing me back toward the sea. I was able to wound him, but his longer arms didn't allow for me to get close enough for a strike on him, much less a killing blow.

He seemed to block out the sun as he towered over me, and then I knew no more.

WHEN I OPENED MY EYES, I HURT. EVERYTHING HURT. MY ENTIRE body screamed in pain. There was something on me, and all around me, and... the battle was still going on. At least I thought it was. I couldn't raise my head. But I could hear the screams and the angry bite of metal on metal. It made me tired, and I couldn't keep my eyes open. A knife bit into my neck, and then I felt... I felt... I didn't know what I felt.

Tired. So tired.

I closed my eyes again. When I opened my eyes once more, it was to clutch at my ruined throat. How could I be so thirsty that it felt like my throat was in flames? I scrabbled to grab at something—anything—my need and thirst making me almost blind. Then something was before my lips, and I drank greedily, the hot, warm liquid sliding down my throat and easing the burning pain.

A blinding light. More pain.

When I closed my eyes for the last time, it was with relief.

CHAPTER ONE

ISABEAU

I laughed as Jonathan twirled me around. We were on spring break in Colorado, and I'd been looking forward to this trip. Not only because he and I would finally have time alone after a demanding final semester at school, but because my best friends were with us. Kari and Tempest joined us outside the condo we'd rented.

"Come on, lovebirds," Tempest said mockingly. "Plenty of time for all that nonsense. Right now, the sun is shining, so let's get our asses up the mountain."

Kari laughed as she added, "I've been watching the weather all week. Today is going to be the perfect day."

"The guide's not even here yet," Jonathan said, setting me down.

We weren't from the area, and backcountry skiing could be challenging. We'd hired a local guide, a man named Chris Knowlton who looked like he was my dad's age, to take us through today.

We'd met him yesterday, and he made us go skiing with him to make sure that we were capable. Me, Tempest, and Kari had been skiing together since we were kids in New England, and later, around Colorado and Utah, but only last year had we gotten into backcountry skiing. Jonathan was probably the most skilled of us, and all four of us had gotten the nod of approval from Chris. We'd gone over backcountry precautions. Chief among them was avalanches. It was the time of year that they were more prone to happen.

As if he knew we were talking about him, Chris pulled up in his battered Explorer. "You ready?" he asked in his gravelly voice.

"Yes!" we all shouted.

Skis and gear loaded up, GPS trackers on, we piled into the Explorer as he took us to one of his favorite spots. We had to hike to get up the mountain. Once we'd reached the point where Chris said it was time to ski, I stood on the top of the mountain, my face turned up to the sun.

It was beautiful.

We began our descent, Chris in the lead. Jonathan was right behind him. I was content to let the two of them go ahead. Today was so gorgeous, I didn't want to just speed down and miss all the things that I enjoyed about skiing.

Tempest blew by me, making me laugh. I sped up a little, chasing her. I turned around to see Kari, who was still behind us, and stopped. My eyes widened as I took in the growing scene that filled my view behind her. The mountains and trees were disappearing. Kari skied toward me unaware.

That couldn't be what I thought it was.

"Avalanche!" I screamed, the day, the sun, everything forgotten. I saw Kari's head whip around and then she shouted at me. Her words were lost in the rumble of the oncoming snow. I watched for a moment, Kari and the snow getting closer, and then I pointed my skis down the hill. I skied faster than I'd ever skied in my life, the roaring behind me closing in. Where was

Kari? I was too afraid to look around to see where she was. She had to be close by. She'd turned, she'd seen it... she had to have.

Oh God oh God oh God oh God! I wanted to close my eyes, stop seeing what I was seeing, but I couldn't. I couldn't. This wasn't real. This couldn't be happening! I saw Tempest ahead of me, but it was hard to make her out with the snow swirling around me.

I could feel the sun disappear as the snow blocked it out, making everything around me cold.

Then a wave of white, and I heard screaming that I didn't recognize as my own. I felt the cold go over my head, and the sounds that had been deafening were now muffled, as though I were far away. My arms went up, fighting to pull me to the top. I remembered that Chris had said try to swim with it, get off to the side. Swim to the side. Swim to the side. My heart thudded loudly in my ears and the cold hurt my throat as my breathing grew ragged. Snow filled my mouth, making me choke. One hand up. Get the snow out. One hand over the mouth. Swim.

Then nothing.

Nothing.

When I woke, the walls were the white of the last thing I'd seen, and I screamed, trying to warn them.

A prick of something sharp stabbed me in my arm. I willingly fell into nothing once more.

CHAPTER TWO

Collum

Present Day

I stared out into the night, listening. I did this every night upon waking, every night for the last five hundred and thirty-five years no matter where I was. I inhaled, taking in the night scents, searching for anything out of the ordinary.

Nothing.

Morag had been scouting just before dawning that morning, and she told me she'd caught a scent that made her shoulders itch. That was Morag speak for an enemy. She wasn't as old as I was, but she was one of our best trackers, and her twitchy shoulders had been right about potential danger more often than not.

I would need to be on the lookout.

It was probably hunters. They came around from time to time. I always tried not to kill them, but it wasn't easy. They were often so blindly determined. Determined that they were right; that I and those like me should die, et cetera et cetera.

From a certain point of view, it made sense. Not my point of view, mind you, but I understood it. As I wasn't ready to die, I had to disagree, and that meant the hunter died. You'd think they would learn. I'd heard they were organized, talking online. That they had discussion boards. Most of us were not interested in world domination, bloodbaths, or anything of the sort. We wanted to be left in peace.

The hunters couldn't abide that, and the conflict continued.

So it has been for the past five hundred years. I don't count the first twenty or thirty years because I was too preoccupied with trying to learn how to be a vampire.

Unlike Margaret, one of the members of my clan, I didn't know who my sire was. In our world, once you made a vampire, you stayed with them, and taught them how to live their new life of immortality. But that hadn't been the case with my sire. Nor the sire of the other members of my clan. Outside of Margaret, we had no idea who our sires were. I had a theory that—

A shadow of movement caught my eye, and I fixated on it, musings forgotten. Whatever or whoever it was, it wasn't moving like an animal. I raced down the stairs from the roof and out into the forest surrounding my castle. I went for where I'd seen the shadow. At the cluster of trees, I stopped, and inhaled deeply again.

A human had been here. A human and... one of us? That was puzzling. Had another vampire come into my territory with their dinner?

It just wasn't done. I huffed in impatience. I didn't want to deal with an ill-mannered asshole.

I'd been human once, when I'd entered into what was now known as Bloody Bay, on the northern side of the Isle of Mull. But now, I lived quietly with my clan, my chosen family, in a restored tower house that had once belonged to my father's cousin. It wasn't a castle, but it had four stories, and to my child's eyes, it had been a palace. In 1720, I was living in England, and I had word that Lochdon House, just southwest of Duart Castle, our clan's seat, was going vacant. My cousin's family had died out in the rising of 1716. I left the vampires I was living with and came back to Scotland for the first time in over one hundred years.

And I'd decided that I'd build my own family; a family of choice, since I couldn't build a family of blood. I didn't know who my sire was. He—or she, although it was more likely it was a he since I had been in the midst of battle when I was bitten and drained—had left me on the beach, trying to hide from the sun, taking refuge under the bodies of my comrades and my enemies. Why my sire hadn't chosen to stay with me was a mystery to this day. I did not know. I'd never met anyone whose blood called to me, spoke to me as family. I'd seen that connection in other clans; that sense of knowing that their shared blood was forever. I craved such a thing for myself.

It was after years of searching, of talking to all the vampires from my time, my part of the world, that I'd decided it didn't matter. Lochdon House becoming vacant had sealed the deal for me.

I would go home and I would create that which I wanted.

Now I had a clan, and family. I didn't have a mate, but... I was fairly certain that wouldn't happen. Not again.

I'd already met her. I'd lost her, by my own hand. While she lived, my heart had beaten in time with hers. When her heart had stopped, so had mine. I had no hope that it would ever beat again.

There would be no more love for me.

I'd accepted it. I sighed and turned my thoughts from the past and focused on following the trail. The vampire was the only one running now. That must mean he or she was carrying the human.

Interesting.

Vampires did not allow themselves to be used by humans.

Not under normal circumstances. Something told me these were not normal circumstances.

I'm going out. Some odd visitors, I thought, focusing on my clansman, Lyall. He would hear me and know to look for me if I should not return prior to dawning.

A grin crossed my face. The hunt was on.

CHAPTER THREE

ISABEAU

I set aside the diary and stared out the plane window. Gran had given me the diary before I left—before she pushed me out the door and onto a plane. She'd told me that it was time that I get out of my house and come back to the world.

The problem was, I didn't want to.

Life was so fragile. It ended in the time it took to blink, and there wasn't a damn thing to do about it. Despite my awareness, I didn't want to die.

But I was afraid to live.

As it did every day, my mind returned to the day that had changed my everything. I didn't want to revisit it, but my memory camera had other ideas. The whole horrible thing replayed in my head at least once a day. At least it was down to only once a day. That was an improvement.

I started in my seat on the plane, bumping my head against the window. I must have dozed off for a moment. I rubbed my eyes and closed the copy of the diary in front of me.

Would that ever go away? That vision of seeing the snow envelop Kari and pull her from my sight? It was bad enough I saw it every night that I tried to sleep. Why did I have to see it when I was awake?

I willed myself not to cry. I was tired of crying. But it was as if my eyes were on a permanent leak setting.

That's why I was here, on this plane flying in the dark night over the Atlantic Ocean.

It was all due to Gran. She had stormed into my parents' house two nights ago.

"Isabeau! It's time to get up!" she'd yelled up the stairs.

I could hear my parents shushing her, and her telling them to go to hell. She thumped up the stairs to where I'd holed up in my room.

"Gran, what?" I asked, rolling over in bed to face the wall.

The air was cooler on my legs as the blankets were yanked off me. "It's time to stop this crap, that's what!"

I turned over, grabbing at them and glaring at her. "That's not for you to decide!"

"Well, if we leave it up to you, you'll be here until we're all dead. Do you think this is what they would have wanted?" Gran stood, her eyes shooting sparks and her hands on her hips as she faced me.

"I don't know what they would have wanted! I'd ask them, but they're not here!" I yelled. "They're not here, Gran! I am, and they'll never be here again!" I burst into tears, unable to keep the anger going.

I felt her sit down on the bed next to me. "Baby." An arm went around my shoulders. "They aren't coming back. You letting yourself rot in here won't change that."

I looked up at her. "You think I don't know that?"

"No." She shook her head. "I don't think you know that at all. I think you think that if you sit here and let your life go to pieces, it will make up for the fact that they aren't here."

"Gran," I began.

"No. Honey, no. I have a little more experience with losing

those I love. I know, I know, not like you do, but when you get to
be my age, dying becomes one of those things you see happen.
And I'll tell you that all the self-hate in the world doesn't do
anything—not for those who have passed, and not for those
who are still here."

I looked at her and started to cry.

"Baby, you have to get this out. And then you have to get on
with the business of life. It's not stopping, no matter how much
you want it to."

"How can I?" I whispered. The guilt lay on me like an anvil.
I was never without it. Everywhere I went, every waking
moment—I heard their voices, the screams, and then the
silence. *They're dead they're dead they're dead* was a constant
refrain. I was able to push it to the side at times, but I was never
without it.

"Issy. If you had been the one who had died, what would
you want for Tempest? Or Kari? Or Jonathan?"

It was hard to hear their names, and yet, I loved hearing
them. I missed them so. It had been the longest year of my life.

"I'd want them to go on living. To live for me," I added, the
words coming out before I was aware of it.

Gran took my hands. "Yes. You loved them. They loved you.
An avalanche is an accident. I know that there were a lot of
accusations thrown around, but in your case, it was an accident.
Chris was experienced, and he'd already been out in that area.
He was confident it was safe. But you can't manage nature, and
that day, nature did what it was going to do. There was nothing
you could have done." She gripped my hands, looking into my
eyes, forcing me to keep eye contact.

Which was tough. I'd been avoiding eye contact, and any
other contact, for the past year.

"Gran, I don't know how to go on without them." None of
this was new territory. I'd heard it all. Been to a therapist a
zillion times.

"No, you don't. And you're not going to learn if you don't get out there and try."

"And do what?" I'd been granted a compassionate waiver for the end of the semester. My diploma had arrived two months after the trip. The degree that had seemed so important, the job that I'd been preparing for—none of it mattered. Not anymore.

"Everything is different, so that means you need to be different too. Forget the job." She waved a hand. "Forget everything you've ever thought about. It's time to go do something else, something you never would have done before."

"Why are you telling me this now?" She hadn't said any of this to me in the past year.

"Because I got up today, and I knew that today was the day I was supposed to come and talk to you. It wasn't time before," she said.

"What does that even mean?" I asked.

"It means that I listen to my gut feeling when it speaks. And today, my gut told me to come see you and drag your ass out of here. Your room smells, speaking of ass. Did you know that?"

I stared at her for a moment and then burst out laughing. My gran was a proper old lady who still wore white gloves in the summer because she liked it and said that it made people treat her with more respect. She didn't swear often, but when she did, it was situations like this.

She joined me, asking, "When did you shower last, young lady?"

I shook my head, still laughing. "I don't know."

"That is *not* the correct answer." Gran stood up, sniffing. "You get your behind into the shower, and then you come downstairs and have some tea and something real to eat with me. And your parents. They are worried sick about you."

"I know," I said, shame washing over me.

"No, no, you don't get to hike yourself further up the martyr cross. There's quite enough of that going around. I'm just letting you know that there are more people than you who are part of this. And it's time for you to come out and be part of the world again."

I got up. The moment my feet hit the floor her arms were around me. I must not have smelled that bad.

"I love you more than you'll ever know," she said. "I'd imagine it's the way you love Tempest, and Kari, and Jonathan. But it's time to let them rest in peace. It's time for you to find peace and live again."

I cried into her shoulder.

"Go shower." Gran let go of me and shoved me out the door toward my bathroom. "Then come see me. And don't dawdle," she called as she went back down the stairs.

I shut the door behind me and leaned against it. The simple act of leaving my room made me breathless. Then I heard Gran in my head. They would all kick my ass if they could see me right now. Even Kari, who was the kindest, gentlest person I'd ever known. They'd be angry at me for wasting the past year.

I stepped into the shower and turned on the water, taking the first steps into not smelling like ass and living again.

Which brought me back here, over the Atlantic at night.

Gran had given me the diary of her great, great, great, great —too many greats for me to keep track of—grandmother. She was Scottish, and she'd been condemned to die by fire because she'd been found to be a witch.

Until she up and disappeared in the middle of the night. Supposedly with her white demon lover.

Gran said that she'd been curious about this her entire life, ever since her mother had given her two diaries—one that was the original diary of Elizabeth Martin that ended the night before she was supposed to die, and the translated version that her mom had done. The original diary was wrapped up in my bedside table at home, but I'd brought the translated version.

I didn't tell Gran, but the original diary made all my nerves jangle. It had been taken and hidden by Elizabeth's daughter and passed down through the family. Or so the family legend said. I would have brushed it all aside as historical wishful thinking, but it made me profoundly uncomfortable to touch it. She'd insisted I take it, though. Something about her insistence made me realize it was better not to fight with her. I couldn't bring myself to pack it, however.

She wanted me to find Elizabeth. Find out what happened to her. See what I could discover.

"You might not find out anything. People didn't like to talk about witches, and now, with all the exposure of the kinds of women that were accused of witchcraft, no one wants to admit their ancestors participated in this sort of thing. But see what you can find."

"Gran, this is a wild goose chase that doesn't really have an end," I complained as I sat at the table with her and my parents.

"So what? I'm bankrolling it, if it is a dead end. And really, Issy, what do you have to do? What, you have to be somewhere?" She rolled her eyes. "I've already booked your ticket, and gotten you a car, and hotels all along the way."

"Is there anything you haven't planned for me?" I asked.

"Given the state of you and your room, I figured you might need a roadmap. I'm hoping you'll learn to do it for yourself again," she shot back.

My mom covered her mouth, trying not to laugh.

We'd all ended up laughing. It was the first time I'd felt like laughing in a year.

Yesterday, before I'd left, I'd gone to see Tempest and Kari's parents. To tell them I was so sorry, again, and that I was leaving to do some family research in Scotland for my grandmother. Kari's mom had burst into tears saying, "Thank God!" as she hugged me.

It made me feel so ashamed. They had lost as much as I

had, and they were worried about me.

I'd also called Jonathan's mom. She had been a bit more reserved but had told me she was glad that I was getting out of the house.

It was stupid, but I didn't feel like I could just leave without talking to the three of them.

And now, here I was.

I looked over the itinerary Gran had prepared for me. Maybe I could actually find out something for her. All I needed to do was follow the path she'd laid out for me.

It dawned on me that perhaps Gran had done this so that I would run my own show, and not merely walk on and off stage. Which was too deep to deal with at the moment. I had a car to pick up, driving to manage, and then churches and parishes galore to visit over the next couple of days.

There was also a ferry ride in there, so I had plenty to manage without diving too deep into Gran's ulterior motives. Besides, if I waited long enough, she would call me and tell me herself, so no point in stealing her thunder.

I looked at the itinerary again. She had put a lot of time and love put into this. It made the tears well up in my eyes. I didn't deserve— No. I stopped myself. I had to stop thinking that way. I dashed at my eyes and looked out the window. Forward. I needed to look forward.

When I landed in Glasgow, I picked up my rental car and carefully made my way out of the airport. It was a good thing, because this driving on the left side would take some getting used to. I was grateful to have flown overnight, so I could drive during the day. I made it to Oban in good time and found that Gran had reserved me and my little car a space on the ferry to a town called Craignure. That wasn't where I was staying, but it was close. It was on the north side of the Isle of Mull.

The ferry ride was less than an hour, and uneventful. It was a much larger ferry than I was expecting, but that added to my feelings of calm and security. I hadn't felt that way in a long time. Odd that I felt it here on the other side of the ocean.

As I got off the ferry and turned to Tobermory, I drove slowly. Remembering the video Gran had sent a link for about driving here—everything was a one lane road—I moved over every time I could, because I knew I was driving like a grandma. Well, maybe not MY Gran, who still got at least one speeding ticket a year.

Tobermory coming into view was beautiful. The houses along the waterfront were neat and different colors, giving everything, even me, a cheerful air. I was staying in a hotel right along the water, essentially. It was the bright pink building, and I figured Gran had to know that. But it made me happy, and I checked in, relieved to be done traveling for a while.

I made my way down to the bar, chatting with the bartender as I ordered a meal. I wasn't ready to dig into the stuff from Gran, and asked Gale, the bartender, what was happening around tonight.

"There's a cemetery tour this evenin'," he said.

The accent here was charming. What I loved was that I wasn't home. Gale directed me to the front desk where I was able to sign up for the tour. After getting instructions on where to meet—the tour guides would drive us, thank god—I went back to nap.

I was refreshed and feeling good when I met the tour down at the clock tower, and we set off in a passenger van.

There were no lights. I was so glad that I wasn't driving. We reached the first graveyard, and I was listening to the guide, wondering if I'd have a chance to look around. I wanted to see the headstones. The light across the street didn't provide much to see by.

A man crashed through the small grove of trees and leaped over the stone wall that ringed the cemetery. My phone dropped from my hand.

CHAPTER FOUR

COLLUM

He was very fast. I felt it was a he, although I had nothing to go on. Vampires don't put off pheromones like humans do. I can not only smell a human a mile away, I can discern the flavor—man, woman, old, young, sick, healthy; your scent gives off a wealth of information to creatures like me.

It is a wonder dogs love humans so much. Something about them must still smell wonderful to dogs. To me, they smelled like food, most of the time. But I loved children, and no child was ever to be harmed on this island ever. I'd laid down the law. Any clansman who harmed a child would be banished. Any guest would be forbidden to return. This was a small island. We couldn't afford to have a vampire go after a child. We were the only clan on the Isle of Mull, and I planned to keep it that way. Usually, most of us went onto the mainland to hunt. Less chance of detection.

Most of those who'd been our guests wouldn't cross our rules, but sometimes a young one would pass through. I remembered those years, always hungry, on the edge of tearing something, or someone apart. With no sire to teach me, I'd had to teach myself. A hundred years or so in a coven in England had helped me, but I would never stop feeling sympathy to the lost young ones. Even if they broke my laws. That didn't mean I would show them mercy, but my sympathy was always there.

Because most new vampires on their own didn't make it. I'd been lucky I had.

Back to the matter at hand.

I slowed, allowing myself to catch the scent. We were moving northwest, toward Tobermory. There would be more people, more civilization. I had to be careful.

The wind shifted, and I caught the scent. Following it, I jumped up onto a rock wall surrounding the Tobermory cemetery, continuing to look around so as to not be surprised by him.

A murmuring on the other side of the cemetery halted me.

Humans.

Shit.

I inhaled deeply, catching the scent of them, hoping to see that he'd tried to mask himself within their numbers.

He wasn't there.

But— I stopped. There was...another scent, one that made me feel I couldn't get enough of it

What was it? I let my head tip back, focusing on the light, intoxicating scent that reminded me of fruit, and florals, and warmth. My heart thumped in a beat so loud I forgot what I was about.

It couldn't be.

The last time my heart had beaten had been over three hundred years ago, when I'd been a vampire for nearly two hundred years. It had started slowly, although not this slow, and it had only stopped when— I shook my head. I didn't want to think about it. I'd already visited my past this evening. I had no desire to visit again.

I moved closer, searching for the source of the scent, to see if my heart would beat again. I didn't want my heart beating to be a true thing – I wanted it to be merely a figment of my imagination. Hoping against hope that my heart had not beaten, merely moved within my chest. Because a heartbeat meant only one thing.

A thing I never wanted to go through again. Never.

The small group stopped, and I could tell all the humans were staring at me. I slowed my hunting instincts, put a smile onto my face, making sure to retract my fangs, and walked toward them, looking for the one who would style themselves the leader.

"Sir? Can I help you?" An older man with a beard and mustache took it upon himself to step forward. His accent suggested he was a local.

One of the women moved closer.

This could go easily, or badly, depending.

I hoped for easily. Even as luck wasn't really with me right now, and Lady Luck was giving me the finger. I gave up on my hunt for the evening, and put a smile on my face.

CHAPTER FIVE

ISABEAU

I reached down to pick up my phone, my fingers searching blindly because I couldn't stop staring at the man who had sort of joined us. His head was thrown back, and he looked like some warrior from a thousand years ago with a sharp, strong profile that was backlit by the evening moon.

His hair was a little longer than what most guys were wearing, because he had it pulled back at the nape of his neck. It was light, so I'd guess a light brown or dark blonde color. I wanted to run my hands through it.

As I stood, I felt my feet bring me closer to him. His head turned, and his gaze fixed on me. His eyes were as dark as the night, and I couldn't stop staring at him. I wanted to be closer, as close as you could get—

"Sir? Can I help you?" Our guide, an older man named Michael, pushed past me, momentarily breaking the spell of the stranger's eyes.

But not the pull of him. I wanted to walk to him— the tour, mission, Gran's itinerary; everything else seemed unimportant.

"I am sorry to disturb you." The man smiled. "I'm Collum

MacLean, from Lochdon House. I lost my... dog. Has one come through here?"

Michael's lips twisted for a moment before his face smoothed into a professional smile. He'd obviously heard of Collum MacLean and wasn't impressed with what he'd heard.

At least, that was my guess. Interesting.

"Long way for a walk," Michael said.

"Indeed. He and I drive round the island, looking to explore new places. No matter how long you've lived in a place, you never know it entirely, do you?" Collum smiled widely, white teeth flashing.

"We've seen no dogs," Michael said abruptly. "If you'll excuse us, we have a schedule to keep."

"Of course." Collum inclined his head. "Thank you for your time."

Michael returned the nod and then spun on his heel and brushed past me. "Come along, people, let's keep going."

With a murmur, the rest of the group followed him like ducklings after their mother. All except me. I lingered, not wanting to leave the presence of the fascinating Collum MacLean.

"You should keep up with your group," his deep voice said gently to me.

It reverberated through my very bones.

"I... uh," I stammered.

He moved with what seemed like unnatural quickness, and he was beside me, his white fingers taking my hand and lifting it to his lips. "Forgive me my forwardness, but have we met before?"

I stared up, stunned by the touch of him. His hand was smooth and cool. I could imagine how it would feel— *Stop it!* I told myself.

"I don't think so," I managed.

"Nevertheless, I am struck by the feeling of having met

you," he murmured. "Could I be so bold as to ask you to join me for dinner?"

"Um... yes. I'm not from here," I added.

"Your accent gives that away," he said, and I could swear there was humor in his voice.

It was hard to tell because my head was swimming with the nearness of him.

"Where are you staying?" Collum continued.

"The Tobermory Hotel, the pink one," I said.

"I know it well. I would be honored if you would allow me to join you tomorrow night, say around seven?"

"Yes," I said.

"What is your name?" He asked.

"Isabeau Saint-Martin," I said.

"It has been my pleasure, Isabeau. Until tomorrow." He let go of my hand and was jumping down off the wall opposite me before I'd even registered that he'd left my side.

The empty space beside me where he'd been made me feel bereft.

Collum disappeared, and I felt like whatever spell I'd been under had broken. I hurried to catch up with the rest of the group.

What in the name of all hell had I done? I'd agreed to go on a date? What was I thinking? I couldn't date. Not even for one dinner. It was... it was out of the question.

I spent the rest of the tour telling myself all the reasons I'd just bail on dinner. This wasn't going to happen. It couldn't. There was no way I was ready, no way it was the right thing for me in any universe.

I had no idea what I'd seen after meeting Collum. Elizabeth Martin could have risen from her grave and cursed us all, and I wouldn't have noticed.

That should have concerned me, but I didn't feel fussed. More bemused than anything else.

And wondering why I'd said yes. I shouldn't have.

When I got into bed, I nodded to myself. I'd just meet him and explain that I was indisposed. That would do it, and I'd put the whole disturbing incident behind me.

But as I lay in the dark, trying to sleep, my thoughts were of nothing but him; dark, all-encompassing, engulfing me. I didn't fight it. I let the thoughts of him carry me off, his voice reverberating around me once more.

CHAPTER SIX

COLLUM

I ran all the way back to the other end of the island, not only because I was on foot, but I needed to burn off the energy that meeting Isabeau had stirred in me.

My heart had not moved in her presence again, but I could feel the pull of her even now. It was there, and though my heart was still for the time being, getting close to her had told me that if, in fact, my heart was beating with a purpose, this was the woman who had caused it.

Which is why I had impulsively asked her out? To see. To know.

But to what end?

Like it was yesterday, I could recall the events of two hundred years ago when I'd met my Sarah. She had been the daughter of a court tailor, and I'd seen her in a tavern, after she and her father had a meal one night. He'd gone home, and she'd stayed to talk to the serving girls. I Even then, young women were not given the freedom to move about on their own.

Then, as now, my heart had begun to beat. But unlike now,

my heart beat, I discovered, in quarter time with Sarah's. From the moment I met her until the moment her heart stopped forever, my heart was always beating in quarter time with hers.

After I'd followed her home on the night I'd seen her, mostly to see if this amazing thing had something to do with her, I hurried back to the nest.

I'd arrived in London over one hundred years before then, at the coronation of King Jamie. James IV he was, now that Elizabeth had passed, and I assumed, rightly, that there would be a great many more people than normal in London. Easier hunting. It was there I met Miles, who even now I'd call one of my friends, and the clan that he lived with.

Unlike me, Miles had spent fifty years with his maker. She'd been killed when hunters attacked their nest, and he'd found himself in London, just as I was.

Most of the nest I lived with was related by blood. Either they were related when human, or they were related by our dark blood. I envied that. There would never be a blood tie for me, unless I made my own vampire children, or took a mate.

So it was to them I went to ask what was happening. Many of them were mated. All of them smiled.

"It would seem you have met your mate," Serina, the de facto leader said. Thomas, her mate, took her hand and smiled.

"Does your heart still move?" he asked.

"It does," I said. "But slower."

Serina nodded. "It will beat now for as long as she lives."

"Really?" I was fascinated.

"Yes," Thomas replied. "You now have two choices. You may stay with her for the entirety of her human life, or you may choose to bring her over."

The enormity of what he said hit me like an axe. I'd had a horrible time of moving from human to vampire. I would not wish that on another—not even my worst enemy. Certainly not on someone I cared for.

"Are you sure?" I asked, taking a few deep breaths of air. I didn't need it, but this conversation made me feel as though I did. "What if she does not return my affection?"

"If she is your mate, she will," Serina said.

"Have you forgotten how to be with a woman?" Thomas asked with a laugh. "Woo her."

"That may be difficult for a Scotch savage," Miles said as he passed by where we stood. "They drag their women off by their hair, and deposit them in huts made of twigs and mud. A good Englishwoman will not be swayed by dirt, be it Scotch or otherwise."

It made all of us laugh, and I felt better, less concerned. I would court her, and then see if I could tell her my truth, if I could convince her to build a life with me. To be of my blood, of my line.

To be my family.

It took me some time to meet her. She did not venture out alone often. Finally, I booked an appointment with her and her father to tailor new clothing for me. I insisted they come to our nest—we had a home for appearances—and they dutifully arrived at the appointed time.

Sarah was as enthralled with me as I was with her. We flirted through all the fittings. When I was able to take her hand, to bring it to my lips—I thought I might explode with desire.

Soon she was meeting me at night, escaping from her house and into my arms.

I'd never been happier.

One night, as we sat on a small rise in a common, she leaned into me. "Tell me your truth, Collum."

"What do you mean?"

"I know that you are not like other men. Tell me your truth."

Her soft voice compelled me, and I told her. Sarah's eyes

widened, and then she took my face in her hand and kissed me. The scent of her, her warmth, her heartbeat—it was as though I were drunk. My fangs extended as she kissed me, and when she ran her tongue over them, I nearly lost all control.

Nearly.

I told her everything. How I'd come to be, how we were fated. But that anything that happened was her choice. And I looked at her, my long dead heart in her hands. Waiting.

"I want to be like you," she said.

"What about your father?"

"He will do well without me. We have a good business, and he will find another girl to work with him."

"He will miss you."

Sarah looked into my eyes. "Not like you would miss me. And not like I would miss you. I cannot live without you, Collum."

We set the date where I would drain her and bring her back to me as a vampire. The night I was able to pierce her neck, drink her sweet blood, and then feed her with my own—I was lost in a maelstrom of hope and happiness. She tasted of sunshine and moonlight and like nothing I'd ever tasted before. It was dizzying. I took her to ground with me, not trusting anyone else to be with her when she woke.

When I emerged from the sleeping hole, I carefully brought Sarah's body out, laying her on a bed, and making sure there was someone for her to feed on nearby. I remembered the painful, burning thirst. She would need to feed immediately. I waited with her all that night, until dawn began to break. Her face had already begun to pale, her cheekbones becoming more prominent, and her lips holding a faint blush of their formerly rosy hue. She was going to be even more beautiful when she woke. When she would be mine.

Sarah did not stir.

I took her to ground with me a second, and then a third day.

Each night, I woke and laid her carefully on the bed I'd prepared.

The door opened and Serina and Thomas came in.

"My friend," Serina said.

"No." I held up my hands, fangs extending, placing myself between them and Sarah.

"She has not risen. Not all who wish to come to our way are able. You must let us help you now," Serina said, her tone still calm but her words firm and unwavering.

"No," I said again.

Thomas took my hands, drawing me from Sarah. "Please, Collum, let us help you. I am so sorry," he said.

"How could this happen?" I whispered.

"It is not for us to say," Serina said. "Not all humans can withstand the change. We do not know why."

"But why my Sarah?" I felt the truth of her words shatter the determined resolve I'd been keeping about me the past two days.

Serina moved to the bed, and I heard the shush of fabric as she began to move Sarah.

"No!" I wheeled around. "I will take her. I will return her to her father. I will see her laid to rest."

"Are you sure?" Serina's dark eyes searched mine.

I'm knew I looked wild and unhinged. I was. But I knew what was right, and I would do right by Sarah.

"I am." I nodded, my teeth grinding.

"Take Thomas with you. And come back," she added. "We are here for you."

I didn't argue. Serina didn't pull rank or assert her leadership often. The rational part of me knew this, even as the rest of me wanted to cry and wail and destroy things.

Thomas followed me as I carried Sarah to her father's house. I put her in the small garden in the back of their home, arranging her on the bench. She looked as though she'd fallen asleep.

"I am sorry, my love," I said. "I am so sorry."

"She left this world knowing of your love," Thomas said. "This was not your fault."

"Wasn't it?" I asked bitterly. "It was my actions that took her life."

"No. We cannot tell who will become a vampire, even as we may desire to be sure."

I hated the calm of his voice but reined in my anger.

Stroking Sarah's hair, kissing her cheek and blushing lips one last time, I followed Thomas from the garden.

Once Sarah was buried, I went to the churchyard to see her grave. A mound of dirt lay over my beloved. I could see small posies of flowers that others had left, and there were prints in the dirt where someone had fallen to their knees.

"I am sorry," I said again. I could feel a tear slide down my cheek.

I had a stone placed on her grave, and for the next two years, I visited her regularly. But I could feel myself going mad, feeling more and more tightly wound, like a top waiting to explode.

The Rising of 1716 saved me. It freed up the house and the land back on Mull, and I was happy to leave London, even as I also left my nest.

But it was time to go home.

I shook my head now, remembering the pain of those years. Even now, the thought of Sarah was a shaft of agony. I'd loved her, and in my wanting to love her, I'd killed her.

There was no chance for me to love again. I'd found my love and killed her.

After her death, I resolved I would never attempt to make another vampire. My clan now was of vampires like me— lacking a sire, a known history. We came together, and built something different, something not made solely of blood links. That was the only way I'd bring another vampire into my clan.

I also found that I was unable to drain a human when feeding. I learned to drink to a point and stop.

No other human would die at my hands ever again. They were already bloody enough.

CHAPTER SEVEN

ISABEAU

I woke to a shaft of sunlight stretching across my bed. I fell asleep with the sound of Collum MacLean's voice in my head. The gentle hum of his accent made all my senses go on high alert.

Tonight, I would have dinner with him. Would it be too forward to— No! I stopped myself, and my traitorous thoughts. What was I thinking?

I didn't even know what I was thinking, honestly. Being around the man had driven all rational thought right out of my head. Probably out of the town limits.

I was being ridiculous.

Today's schedule included me taking my car and going to a couple of church parishes, to check registers. Gran warned me that record keeping was spotty at the time, but something as notorious as a witch trial would have been news worth recording.

Part of me wanted to ask around, but the thought of exposing my poor ancestor all over again made me uncomfortable.

So trudging to churches it was.

Getting out of bed, I thought about the route I planned to take today. I wasn't going to go to Dervaig, where Elizabeth was from. Not quite yet. Thoughts of dinner tonight were deliberately pushed aside. Collum MacLean was absolutely drop dead gorgeous, and I'd nearly turned into a blubbering pile of goo in his presence—but he wouldn't be anything permanent. I wasn't looking for someone new, and certainly not a vacation fling.

Best to think of him this way and make it a little easier for me to send him on his way. I'd try to split the check with him—that would make my intentions clear and maybe make it easier to get rid of him.

I nodded to myself in the shower. It was as sound a plan as any. The fact that my heart wanted something else, and my body wanted even more of that something else, didn't matter.

I was in charge. The heart and body would have to fall in line and do what was best for all of us.

My plans took me to the opposite end of the island, to the historical centre, and the ruins at Iona. That last one was just for fun, but it was beautiful.

There were several references to witch accusations that directed me to two different churches, one of which was in Dervaig. It was built after Elizabeth Martin's time, but the historical centre suggested that records might have been moved there.

The whole thing felt a little muzzy. I had nothing better to do.

By the time I returned to my hotel, it was time for me to take a shower. I considered what to wear. I hadn't brought anything I'd think of as 'date clothes'—which was good, since this wasn't really a date, and I'd be ending it as soon as I politely could.

However, I didn't want to look like a bum, so I chose one of my nicer pairs of jeans, and a light blue sweater. I liked the way it went with my hair. Being a redhead meant you had certain colors that worked—and those were the colors you stuck with.

I went downstairs right before seven. The woman at the desk called me over. "Miss Saint-Martin, there's a gentleman waiting for you in the lounge. He asked to make a reservation for dinner. I made one for him but wanted to see if that was all right with you." The woman's face was earnest and her eyes wide.

"Tall, long hair, pale and completely hot?" I asked.

She nodded. "His name is Collum MacLean, and his family owns Lochdon House down the other side of the island. They've been there for ages. He's quiet, keeps to himself."

It was my turn to nod. "I am expecting him. Thank you for your consideration, though."

She smiled. "Us women have to stick together, love."

"I agree. Well..." I smiled brightly, although my insides were dancing. "I'm off."

"Enjoy dinner, Miss Saint-Martin."

"Thank you." I continued on into the lounge.

Collum stood before the fire, turning as I walked in.

"Isabeau, I am glad you are joining me for dinner," he said, his lips, which were lush and red in comparison to his pale complexion, curving into a smile that threw all of my earlier resolutions right out the window.

"Th—thank you for the invitation." I couldn't believe I was stammering.

"Would you like a cocktail before dinner?" His hand encompassed the small bar on the other side of the room.

"No, I think I'm okay," I said.

He took my arm and tucked it into his, leading me to the small dining room. Collum had to duck his head to enter, and he gave his name to the bartender, who led us to a tiny table in the corner next to the fireplace.

"Would you prefer the fire side?" he asked, holding out the chair.

"Yes, that would be nice," I said. Could I be any more lame? Did I care? I was ending this as soon as possible.

Later.

He slid into his seat, moving in one smooth motion. How did he do that, being as tall and big as he was? I didn't remember him being this big—he was like a warrior. The same impression I'd had of him yesterday. He was wearing a sweater and jeans as well, and I could see the outline of his biceps through it.

He was huge. What would it be like to be wrapped in his arms?

I mentally slapped myself. I was still... I hadn't gotten past what had happened to me in the last year, and I still loved Jonathan. This wasn't anything; it was just physical lust. Yes. That made sense. Lust. Physical need. My brain might not be ready for anything or anyone, but my body had been used to a healthy life behind closed doors—that was it.

I leaned back a little, satisfied.

"What brings you to Mull?" Collum asked.

His voice washed over me like a warm wave. I wanted to just drift in it.

"I'm doing some family research," I said.

His eyebrows went up. I got the sense he was genuinely surprised.

"That wasn't the answer I was expecting." Collum confirmed my impression. "I would have thought you a hiker, an outdoorswoman."

"I... I am. Well, I was. Not recently, but..." I stopped, looking away. "I was." I faced him, putting a smile on.

"What happened?" His voice lowered, encouraging confidences.

Did I want to share this? This wasn't first date material.

"Oh, it's a long, sad tale," I said, trying for casual.

Collum folded his hands together, placing them on the table as he leaned forward. "I'd love to hear it," he said.

That voice. It was like honey. I was the bee.

The waiter came by. "Mr. MacLean, miss, good evening. I'll take your drinks order now, if you like. Your usual, Mr. MacLean?"

Collum nodded. He glanced at me. "Are you a drinker of whiskey?"

"I like it," I said.

"Make it two." He nodded to the waiter.

The waiter left, looking happy.

"What did I just order?" I asked.

"I keep a few bottles of my private stock here for when I'd like a drink," he said. "It's from the Tobermory Distillery, and it's a sherried whiskey, thirty-two years old." At my blank look, he laughed. "My apologies. I do tend to rattle on about whiskey. And I enjoy supporting our local distillery."

"Then I'm glad I let you do the ordering," I said.

"Choose your meal," he said, indicating the menu. "Then we can continue this interesting conversation."

I looked down at the menu in some confusion. Talking with Collum was both easy and intense. Our words seemed simple, but I could feel the undertow of something else in the conversation.

Neither of us spoke until the waiter returned. He set down two tulip-shaped glasses in front of us.

"For dinner?" he asked.

"The roast beef," I said.

Collum waved him away when asked for his order.

"You're not eating?"

"I ended up eating earlier with my family," he said smoothly.

"You live with your family? You're married?" I asked.

Collum laughed. "No, not at all. That would make this pretty uncomfortable, wouldn't it?"

I laughed with him, and some of the tension broke.

"I have cousins that live with me, and their spouses. We've all lost our parents." An undecipherable expression flitted across his face. "And we decided that the house was perfect for all of us."

"That's really nice," I said.

"You? Siblings? Family?"

"I'm an only child. Which means my parents are totally up in my business, and my grandmothers, and..." I threw my hands out. "Everyone."

He laughed again. I liked the sound of it. Like his voice, it warmed and surrounded me.

"It was because of Gran—my dad's mom—that I'm here."

"I'm glad," Collum said. Then he stopped. His eyes flashed, a streak of light in their darkness.

"So am I." I took a sip of the whiskey to cover the welling emotions that threatened to overwhelm me.

There was a pause in the conversation. Collum picked it up. "What are you looking for here?"

Now that I was here, and feeling the sense of history all around me, Gran's request didn't seem so far out there. "My great, great something was accused of being a witch. She was condemned to burn at the stake, and the night before her execution, she disappeared. She left a diary." I shrugged. "And my gran wanted to know if it was true, if there were facts that could back up some of the stuff in the diary."

Collum leaned even closer to me over the table. "That's really interesting. When did this supposedly happen?"

"Fifteen hundred? A little later?" I found that I couldn't remember. I didn't want to think about Elizabeth Martin.

His head cocked. "Here on Mull?"

I nodded. "In Dervaig." I remembered that much, at least.

"It's possible. Although the island was not a victim of witch mania like the mainland," he said.

"Are you into history?" I asked.

He blinked and then sipped his drink. "My family has been here for hundreds of years. We're all into history here," he added wryly. "Are you on university break?"

I sobered immediately, his intoxicating presence not enough to stop the cold wave of reality. "I've been on break for a year or so," I said, looking away from him. His intense gaze made it impossible for me to stop talking, and I wasn't sure I wanted to tell him about my personal hell.

CHAPTER EIGHT

Collum

This was it. I could feel it. The air around her changed. My heart, which had been thumping occasionally as we sat and talked sped up. This was the reason she was here, regardless of whatever her research project was.

I'd decided to keep the date, just to get this out of my system, and I found myself sitting with her, basking like a cat in the sun in her presence. Her red hair was lovely in the dimly lit room, and her pale complexion glowed in the firelight.

This wasn't getting her out of my system by any means.

"Doing what?" I asked casually. She wasn't meeting my eyes, and that meant, to me, that she was feeling the effects of my interest. It was hard not to glamor her—when I felt this strongly, the glamor effect leaked out.

But she was resisting. I kept my smile to myself. She was strong. I liked that.

Isabeau sighed and met my eyes. Yes. Very strong.

"Avoiding life," she said.

"Why?"

"Do you really want to know? It's not pretty, and really, not a date kind of story." She spoke as though she'd made some kind of decision.

"I do." I found myself drawn to her even more.

Isabeau leaned back and looked over my shoulder. I stayed quiet, waiting. Waiting wasn't a problem for me.

"Last year, during spring break, I went to Colorado with my friends and my fiancé. We made plans to go backcountry skiing, hired a guide, everything." She looked at me then, and I could see the shimmer of tears in her eyes. "It was one of the most gorgeous days I've ever seen. Blue, clear skies, and the snow sparkled. We started to ski, with Jonathan and Chris heading down first. They were the fastest skiers," she added, her gaze going unfocused.

I knew she wasn't seeing me in that moment.

"I heard something, and I turned around, and there it was. A wall of snow with the gorgeous blue behind it coming down on us. I screamed—I remember that—and I tried to get off to the side, like Chris had talked about. I remember my hand going over my mouth, and then I don't remember anything."

"You survived," I said. "What about your friends?"

She took a breath, and a tear slipped down her face. I didn't think she was even aware. As though someone else was directing my actions, I reached across the table and touched my finger to her face, catching the tear.

Isabeau jumped at my touch.

"They didn't make it," she said, her face ravaged at the words.

"I am so sorry," I said.

"I've spent the last year hiding out. My gran dragged me out and tossed me on a plane and gave me something to do." The words came out in a rush.

"Is it helping?" I asked.

She shrugged. "I don't know. Meeting you—" She stopped. "That wasn't part of the plan."

"I hope it's a positive addition?" I asked, keeping my tone light.

"Yes, and no. I have so much baggage I have my own personal baggage cart," Isabeau said. She sounded annoyed.

"Everyone has a baggage cart," I said.

"Really? Even you? What are you? Twenty-five? How much baggage can you have?"

I forgot, sometimes, that I'd become immortal at the age of twenty-six. I still looked like my young self, centuries be damned.

Maybe I needed to get out more.

Maybe I needed to deal with whatever this was becoming and then think about getting out more.

"More than you'd think," I said. "Regardless, I am sorry. What a horrible thing to live through."

Her anger dissipated like the ebbing tide. "I'm barely living. I don't want to die, but I'm afraid to live."

"Why?" I understood this. My entire life had changed after Sarah. Some things did that to you, human or immortal.

"Because life can be gone in an instant."

"Isn't that the truth," I said before I could check myself.

"You get it, then?"

"I do."

She sagged in what looked like relief, if I was reading her emotions right.

"No one else does. I just need to get back out there, I can't stay in my room, I can't let myself die, I have to, I have to, I have to!" Her voice rose for a moment, and then she lowered it, looking around as she did so. "I don't know what the hell I want to do. My entire life, all the people who I'd thought would be part of it forever—they're gone. And I don't know what to do." The last words came out as barely a whisper.

I reached across the table and took her hand. "I understand."

"How?"

"I've lost... I've lost my most beloved family members to violence," I said. This wasn't a conversation I had normally, so I wasn't completely smooth on trying to describe my loss of immediate family.

"It sucks," Isabeau said.

The waiter chose that moment to return with her beef, and she let go of my hand, but her thumb caressed mine as she took her hand back.

Lust raged through me like a wildfire. My heart beat a little faster at the touch of her, at the charged atmosphere. This woman was a fighter, and she was strong, so strong—she had reserves she didn't even know about yet. And she had the experience of one much older.

I hated to admit it. I didn't want to. But there was a reason this woman made my heart beat.

"Are you sure you don't want something to eat?" she asked, her fork poised over her plate.

"I'm fine, thank you. I didn't plan on eating, but my family had plans I didn't know about, so I decided to spend time with them and then with you."

"Thank you," she said. She took a bite of her food.

For a few moments, we sat in silence. Unlike earlier, this was less awkward. More comfortable, the whole sexual tension piece aside. I wanted to tear her clothes off and have her in my bed, but that would need to wait.

No. This couldn't happen. I would not be the reason another woman died. I steeled myself for breaking this off gently.

Unfortunately, I'd already made it harder on myself. And her.

"Thank you for sharing with me," I said suddenly.

"Well, I can't say that I'm glad, but I am glad," Isabeau said. "I don't like to talk about it. But you make it easier."

"Thank you," I said again. She was making this even more difficult.

"I don't know why, but you do," Isabeau looked at me.

I found her pain, her suffering, intoxicating. Not that I took pleasure it in. No. This was someone who understood, who had lost, as I had.

She was changed by her pain.

"How old are you?" I asked.

"Twenty-two. Almost twenty-three."

She was a good fit for me.

I had to stop this. While every moment I spent with Isabeau was better than the last, and my heart was beating regularly, although not steadily, in her presence, this was not going to go any further. I would not make another vampire, even if the human wanted me to. In talking with Isabeau, I had no idea whether she'd want me to. She was drawn to me. I could feel

that. Even with this short amount of time. Much like I was drawn to her. The mate attraction assured that.

There was nothing that said you had to accept your mate. Her life would be better—safer—without me in it. Although I didn't know anyone who'd turned from the mating bond. However, I'd already killed once when I attempted to offer immortality. My track record pretty much sucked.

"And you?" she asked, dragging me from my own sad thoughts.

"Oh, I'm twenty-six," I said.

Isabeau smiled, the movement changing her face, and making me think of the sun coming out. Even though I'd not seen it for over five hundred years, she was the sun come to life in front of me. I took a breath, which was a mistake.

She smelled delicious. All my senses were attuned to her, even more so once I'd smelled her. God, I wanted her. I wanted her blood, her body—all of it.

"You okay?" she asked.

I nodded. "So is it working? This trip, I mean?"

The smile was replaced by a frown, but the frown was more thoughtful than sad. "I don't know,

honestly. When Gran came bursting into my room, I was profoundly ungrateful. Now, I think I'm glad. But..." She stopped. "After I've spent the last year trying to escape life, it's kind of hard."

"It can be. I'm sorry this year has been so tough," I said, reaching across the table to take her hand again. Touching her was like touching a live electric wire. It thrilled me in a way I'd not felt in years.

She jumped slightly, which I might not have noticed if I were human.

"What are you doing to me?" she whispered.

"Probably what you're doing to me," I said, deciding it was time to stop ignoring the elephant in the room. To hell with the shoulds and should nots.

"I don't know if I'm ready for this," she said.

"For what?"

"Whatever this is." Isabeau withdrew her hand from mine.

She was anxious saying that. I could feel it in her heartbeat, which had become part of my background noise already. My heart thumped once, twice. I wondered why it was so much less regular and slower than before. I wished I had someone to ask, but I didn't. After I'd left the London coven, the rest of the vampires had gone their own way. I hadn't spoken with Serina or Thomas in nearly one hundred years. No one had.

But I remembered what Serina told me. That the mating process was different for every vampire—no one would be the same. I supposed that held true if one was lucky enough to find two mates.

It didn't matter, I told myself. It didn't matter how delicious I found Isabeau on every level. Or how meeting someone like her, who knew pain and loss, who would understand mine, I realized—it didn't matter.

I wasn't going to take this any further.

"It doesn't have to be anything, if you don't want it to," I said.

"I think I'm full," she said, pushing her plate away. I noted that she'd eaten almost everything.

"Would you like to walk a bit?"

"Yes," she said.

I took care of the bill and we walked out into the night together. I always enjoyed being by the shoreline. There were a great many more smells, but the harbor of Tobermory smelled like home to me, even after all these years.

Without thinking, I caught up her hand and wove my fingers into hers. We moved off away from the hotel, neither of us speaking. I thought she might pull her hand away, but she didn't. My desire for her was growing, and I could feel my fangs extend.

How I wanted this woman. My heart thumped twice as if in agreement.

"Thanks for listening," Isabeau said suddenly. "I don't talk about it a lot."

"I'm happy to. I understand loss. It changes you."

She looked up at me, and her hand tugged at mine, slowing our pace. "Yes! That's what it is, and I haven't been able to explain it. People keep talking to me like I'm the person I was before all this happened, and I'm not." She looked down. "I don't even know who that is anymore."

I stopped, bringing her close to me. "The change you're experiencing doesn't have to be bad," I said.

"It feels like it," Isabeau replied.

My hand came up as though someone else was directing it and stroked her cheek down to her jaw, and then her neck. She straightened, and her head fell back, exposing her neck to me. I could see the blood pumping along her neck, could feel the thud of her blood moving in her veins, and my cock swelled as I took in her scent. She wanted me.

It was like drinking too much too fast, and for a moment, my composure snapped. My other hand came up to cup her face, and I took a step closer to her as my mouth found hers.

CHAPTER NINE

Isabeau

His cool lips on mine made the blood race through me. Warmth bloomed between my legs, and I could feel my nipples tighten at his touch. It was like every part of my body that had anything to do with sex was dying for this man's touch.

Because I was.

Twining my arms around his neck, I stood on my toes to get closer to him. With a sound that was a cross between a grunt and a moan, he pulled me tightly to him, intensifying his attack on my mouth.

I was ready for it. I wanted it. The warrior vibe I'd gotten from him was out in full force, and I was the enemy ship, ready to be boarded. Plundered. Taken.

No man had ever kissed me like this before.

His tongue thrust into my mouth in a way that made me want to wrap myself around him. My heart pounded in my ears, and his hands slid down to my butt, cupping me in such a way that I felt every inch of his erection pressed against me.

Oh my God, did I want him.

I blinked as he pulled away from me. The surrounding air, which had just felt so heated and full was now cold.

"What is it?" I asked, still trying to catch my breath. I couldn't hear anything over my heart, and my body was screaming for him to touch me again.

"I need to go," Collum said. His voice sounded ragged. It wasn't the smooth, low timbre I'd been hearing all evening.

"Now?" I asked before I could stop myself.

"Yes, now. Thank you for dinner, Isabeau. I enjoyed it." Without another word, Collum stepped past me and started walking back to the hotel.

Without me.

I watched him, my mouth falling open. What in the ever-loving name of all hell had just happened? Something had, that was for sure. He was into me, as much as I was into him. I could feel the repressed power in his touch, like he was holding back, but only just barely.

So why had he just left?

Looking down, I shook my head to clear it. When I looked up—my eyes seeking Collum because I wasn't going to let him just walk away—he was gone.

How had he left so quickly?

Oh. Oh my God. My hands came up to my mouth. He really didn't want me. I'd thrown myself at him, and this was his way of extracting himself from an awkward situation.

That I'd created.

No. I shook my head again. I hoped no one was watching. I'd look like a crazy woman. Cats would start to wander behind me. He was into me. I might be one big hot mess right now, but he was into me.

But did it matter? I'd been telling myself that I didn't want this, even if I wanted to see him naked. And boy, howdy, did I want to see him naked. That guy was absolutely luscious. The fact that it had been well over a year since I'd even thought about sex, much less wanted it, showed me just how completely Collum had woken up that side of things.

I guess, in the big picture, that was good, right?

Well, not if I was left to manage it alone. I glared in the direction Collum had disappeared. He seemed like such a gentleman! How the hell did a gentleman leave a lady hanging?

Scowling, I marched back to the hotel. Once safely inside my room, I threw myself on the bed, feeling very put upon.

When I finally crawled between the sheets, *alone*, I thought rebelliously, I dreamed of Collum. Of rolling in silken sheets with him, the moonlight coming in through a window in the stone wall near the bed. He licked and nipped at me, the shock of his teeth on my skin making me gasp and want him more.

The sun on my face the next morning, however, confirmed that dreams aside, I was still very much alone.

I lay in bed, considering.

I'd been alone for a long time now. A year wasn't all that long, but it felt like a century when it wasn't planned. So what if Collum had walked away?

I'd been planning on doing the same thing. He just beat me to it.

Tossing back the blankets, I headed for the shower. I was going to make the most of today and put Collum MacLean on the back back burner. With my thanks for waking me up below the waistline.

Full of self-righteous purpose, I hurried through breakfast, and got out the map. My GPS was kind of spotty. Not that I really needed it. It was essentially an island with one big road. But there were little roads shooting off the big one, and I didn't want to get lost. Again, not that I'd get that lost. The island wasn't that big.

There were ten churches still active on the island, and I had four more days here. Then I was off to Edinburgh to look through the National Records. Today it would be the two here in town, and then the one in Dervaig, where Elizabeth was from. If I was feeling good, I'd add in another one.

I was enjoying my daily excursions around the villages of the island. Coming from New England, I was used to small villages, but there was something different here. I loved the countryside. I loved the island.

Gran had insisted that I spend some time here, even after I told her I thought it would be a dead end.

It might be a dead end, but she was right to insist. Not that I'd tell her that. Well, not yet anyway.

At the end of the day, I'd been to the three churches I planned, and found some interesting information, but nothing that related to Elizabeth. Driving through Dervaig was weird. The Bellachroy Hotel was built in 1608. I went in and had a late lunch, and it was strange to think that Elizabeth might have walked through here. Maybe the trial was held here? I'd read about inns and pubs being places to hold trials if there was no courthouse readily available.

But I wasn't able to find anything about her, and I didn't have any major revelations, or flashes of insight, or a run-in with her ghost.

I was glad to make my way back to Tobermory and the pink hotel. As I walked in, the woman behind the desk, the same one who'd been on last night when Collum came in, looked up and smiled at me.

For one brief second or two, I hoped he'd come in looking for me, or left a message. But when she looked down at her work once more, hope fled.

As I fell into bed that night, I thought about him. Tried not to, but my treacherous brain wasn't having it. Neither were all my lady bits, who really wanted to think about him a lot.

"No sense if he's not going to do anything about it," I said crossly to myself.

I could feel cats coiling in the shadows, waiting for me to turn the crazy cat lady corner.

The next day was a repeat of the one before. Drive out to churches, enjoy the scenery, talk to some nice people, get ogled more than I wanted to, and come home to eat everything in sight before I went up to bed.

But something changed over dinner. I sat at a table in the restaurant—not the one by the fire, no way, my back was to that table!—and a chill came over the room. As though someone had left the window open in winter.

A man stood in the doorway; a man dressed in all black. He was wearing leather, which creaked as he came into the small room.

I struggled to keep my face neutral. Leather? Really? He was a little much.

The cold rushed over me as he halted in front of my table. "Miss Saint-Martin. May I join you?" His voice was smooth, like clear water over ice. And just as cold. He was polite, for all that his getup screamed motorcycle-gang-gone-wild.

"Have we met?" I asked. Something about him was off, was seriously creepy.

"We have not. But we have a mutual... friend, I believe."

"I doubt that," I said.

"Oh? Are you not friends with Collum MacLean?"

"Him? No. I've met him. We had dinner. But that was it," I said, my heart racing. Technically, all that I said was true. Any other thoughts I had on the man were none of Creepy's business. "I'm sorry, I don't believe you told me your name," I added.

"I am Fergus. Fergus MacDonald," he said. "But I am called Fergus Mac."

"Well, Mr. Mac, I am really sorry. But Collum MacLean isn't my friend, and I can't help you." Every moment that this guy stood here my heart raced faster. He scared the shit out of me.

There was something in him that hinted at violence and destruction barely contained, even though he didn't make any threatening moves, and didn't raise his voice.

He stared at me, and then bowed, an oddly formal gesture for a guy who looked like a misplaced Hell's Angel. "Of course. My apologies for disturbing your dinner. Good evening."

He walked away, and I watched. He was smooth and easy in his movements. The way that a predator who knew it could kill all in its path moved.

I forced myself to finish my meal. Once I got up to my room, I wasn't coming back. Not now. I was officially creeped out. Skipping dessert, I took the stairs two at a time back up to my room.

I locked the door and leaned against it. I was debating the merits of a bath when a hurried banging on my door made me nearly jump out of my skin.

"Isabeau! Isabeau! Please, open the door!"

It was Collum.

I yanked open the door.

"What?" I asked, officially annoyed.

CHAPTER TEN

COLLUM

I gathered her in my arms before she could say another word and kissed her. I'd run all the way here, not trusting a car to get me here fast enough.

Kissing her, running my hands over her cheeks, through her hair. She kissed me back with equal fervor, which was more than I deserved after going radio silent for the past two days.

I'd had to. I couldn't risk her.

But when I'd felt her fear—I couldn't be stopped. I left the rest of my coven gaping at me as I nearly flew out the window and up the hill behind our home to get to Isabeau.

She was in danger. Grave, deadly danger.

It had passed on from her by the time I made it to the hotel. Common sense would dictate that I stop, turn around, and leave her alone.

I had the common sense of a chicken at this point and raced up to her room, banging on her door.

To find myself here, with her wrapped in my arms, wrapped around me, and with a bed nearby.

Perhaps she was still in grave, deadly danger.

Isabeau pushed me away. "Wait a minute! Wait just one damn minute! What is going on here?" She took a step back and crossed her arms.

I might not have been mated, but as a man who had been walking upright for over five hundred years, I knew the gesture well. I cast a quick glance at the bed; sadly, that wasn't looking like it was going to happen. Hopefully, I'd snuck a look fast enough that she hadn't noticed.

"Don't look around my hotel room like you're going to get to stay!" Isabeau flared at me.

She'd noticed.

Better to take this head on. "What happened to you just now, Isabeau?"

"What do you mean?"

"You were frightened."

Her mouth opened. I didn't think she'd been expecting that.

"I... I was. How did you know?"

"What frightened you—" I broke off. "Hold still, please."

"What the hell? Hold still? Like I'm a dog? Listen, Mr. High-and—"

I covered her mouth with one finger. "Please hold still. Let me see something, and then you may resume telling me about myself in all the detail you wish." I leaned in closer to her, inhaling deeply.

There it was.

Another vampire had been near her, very near her. Near my Isabeau. Near my— Well, she wasn't my anything, and he shouldn't have smelled her on me. It had been forty-eight hours since I'd held her close. Give or take fifteen minutes or so.

She bit at my finger. I was so busy trying to place the scent that she nearly got me.

"Hey! Easy! I'm not trying to hurt you!"

"That makes one of us!" She glared. "And it's none of your business who I see!" Her cheeks flushed.

It was something to do with me. The thought hit me, watching her. Whatever had happened had something to do with me.

"What happened, Isabeau?"

Her lips pursed as she looked away. Then she blew the breath out that she'd been holding and looked at me.

"A truly creepy guy. He said his name was Fergus Mac, Fergus MacDonald, and he was looking for you. He thought, for some reason, that I would know. Like we were friends or something."

"We are friends," I said quickly.

"Oh, sure, right. I haven't heard anything from you the last two days. Great friends." She rolled her eyes.

I didn't know the name. But he was a vampire, and he knew me. "Isabeau, did he seem dangerous?"

She made a huffing sound. "Yes. He was creepy, and he scared me to death. If this is your kind of friend, I'm better off not hearing from you."

"What happened?" I asked, taking her hands in mine. They were cold, and she looked shaken.

"Who is Fergus MacDonald? Why does he want to find you?"

I thought quickly. "I don't know," I said slowly. "That's not an unusual name here in the isles, but I don't personally know anyone with that name." I was telling the truth. I couldn't think of anyone.

"Well, he knows you," she said, wrapping her arms around herself, her face pale. Her hair glowed like a flame against her paler-than-normal skin.

"I am so sorry that this happened to you because of me," I said. I didn't know who Fergus MacDonald was but I would. And soon. "What can I do for you, now?"

"I don't know," Isabeau shook her head. "I feel scared, and I'm scared to go out, or go to my room, or anything."

"Come to my home," I said, the words coming out before my brain had a chance to stop them. "You'll be safe with me and my family."

"I couldn't," Isabeau said even before I'd finished my sentence.

"Yes, you can. We aren't around during the day, so you would have the run of the house, and I have a couple who helps take care of the grounds who would be willing to drive you around."

"I don't know," she said, hugging herself tighter.

"Whatever you want. We can accommodate you."

"What are you, lord of the manor or something?"

"My family has been on this island for hundreds of years. We've owned Lochdon House for nearly three hundred years. I know the families. Not a lot of moving on Mull," I added.

She stared at me for a long moment. Then she sighed. "I'd feel better if I could be around people who knew some crazy had tracked me down and invaded my space."

"My entire family will protect you." My voice came out hard. My fangs dropped down, but I retracted them quickly.

Isabeau looking up, hearing the steel in my words. "You sure about that?"

I nodded. "Yes."

She sighed again. I wasn't really fond of all the sighing, as though she were settling. Then I checked myself. I was pretty certain she was finally feeling a little more in control of her life, and this must have felt like losing it again. So I got over my own selfish reaction and focused on Isabeau.

"Let me pack."

"Would you like some help?"

"No. Just wait here with me." She moved into the room, and I edged closer to the door, giving her the space. I liked seeing her bend and move in front of me. I tried really hard to ignore the fact that her arse was shapely and fit. This really wasn't the time for ogling. No matter how hard it might be, or what was right before my eyes.

When I heard the luggage zippers, I looked down at her. "Ready?"

She nodded.

"Good. Let me drive your rental," I said. I didn't want to talk about why or how I'd showed up without a car.

"What about your car?" she asked immediately.

"I'll have Ned come over and get it. It's not a worry," I added. "And you're still shaken. Let me brave our roads at night."

Isabeau laughed unexpectedly. "Gran told me I'd have to get used to the roads. I watched a video, but it didn't really prepare me. I've been making sure I get back here before dark because I think it just might finish me off."

I laughed with her, and we left together. She felt good, right, next to me. I liked it, feeling like a couple. Mates.

As I stowed her luggage in the boot and got into the car, Isabeau had already buckled herself into the passenger side. I started it and moved slowly out of the town. For the first ten minutes, neither of us spoke.

"What have you been up to for the past two days?" Isabeau asked. Her tone was very casual, too casual.

I'd been a jerk. I knew it. "Work has caught up with me. Sometimes things come up on the estate that need immediate attention." Complete bullshit but it sounded good.

"Oh. Well, I hope everything is all right," she replied.

"It will be," I said. *I hope*, I thought. I'd been trying to stay away from her, but her heart making mine beat had been a constant reminder that a woman who was meant for me was on the isle. I'd felt her even as I slept in the day. She was my waking thought, and my last thought before dawning.

Now that she was coming with me, to my home, I hoped everything would be all right.

I called to Lyall, one of the members of my coven, in my

head. *I'm bringing a human back with me. This is important. Prep for having her in the house.*

A human? I could hear the surprise even through the mental connection.

Yes. She is in danger because a vampire named Fergus MacDonald approached her tonight looking for me. I don't recognize the name, but I smell him on her.

I'll get the others ready. And we'll find out who he is.

I felt the connection go silent. He was the only one who could talk to the rest of us this way, but it was extremely useful. Now the rest of the coven would be aware, and they'd already be looking for the bastard MacDonald. He'd threatened my human. To know that we were connected, he had to have been watching her, watching us. He had to know that I'd spent time with her. We weren't mated and hadn't shared blood. So he was watching her. I blanched at the thought. I'd put her in danger.

Which is why it was best she was coming to Lochdon House.

I glanced at Isabeau. She leaned her head back and closed her eyes. She didn't seem happy, and while I understood, I hoped that if she spent time in my home, saw my life and my fam— No! What the hell was I thinking? I didn't want her to see anything. She was young, with all her life ahead of her.

I'd not take that away from her, or even risk her losing her life and all that was in her future

Never again.

I turned off the main road and up the long driveway that led to my home on the hill. I loved Lochdon House. Because I'd been able to purchase it soon after the heirs had died, I'd been able to preserve a great deal of MacLean history.

We'd modernized, of course, but at its heart, Lochdon House was still a 17th century stronghold. I loved it.

All the lights shone from the windows, and I sent a thank you to Lyall. He'd done it up right in preparation for the human. Plus, under the low, warm lights, our paleness was less obvious.

"Will your family be all right with this?" Isabeau asked, looking up at the house through the window.

"Of course. It's a huge house. There are ten of us, and plenty of empty bedrooms."

"This is gorgeous," she said.

"Thank you. I'm inordinately proud of my home, so I will happily take your admiration," I teased, wanting to find the easy banter we'd had before.

"It's amazing this house is almost three hundred years old."

"It's actually closer to four hundred. Three hundred sixty-eight. My branch of the family bought the house after the Rising of 1715. The branch of MacLeans who had built it had not survived the Rising."

"That's really sad," Isabeau turned to look at me then.

I shrugged, although she was right. "These things happen with rebellions that go poorly." I parked the car. "I'll get your luggage and introduce you to everyone."

"They're all here?"

"It's early still. So, yes." I stopped myself. I'd almost said too much. We usually met for a bit before everyone headed out. They'd still been there when I left to discover what had happened to Isabeau. After I'd called Lyall, none of them would have left.

I hadn't told anyone about Isabeau. Afraid of hearing the truth, no doubt. For me to bring anyone home, much less a human, was something that had never happened. They wouldn't leave until she did, I thought with a silent laugh.

"Ready?" I asked.

"I guess. Why do I feel like I'm walking into the lion's den?"

I laughed out loud a little then, offering her my arm. "These are friendly lions," I said

"But they're lions, nonetheless?"

I smiled, not wanting to laugh at her very accurate assessment. I wondered if she'd feel the difference. Not all humans could—most were not aware of us. That was by design. But some of them...they weren't sure what it was, but some could tell the differences in us.

Thankfully, it wasn't many.

"They can be," I said, opening the front door. "But they're my lions, if that makes a difference."

"I hope so," Isabeau said. The way she spoke, I wasn't sure if I was supposed to hear it.

CHAPTER ELEVEN

ISABEAU

I held my breath as Collum walked through the door. I wanted to hide behind him, and I hadn't been kidding when I said I felt like I was walking into a den of lions.

I think his entire family was ranged out in the hall. Like, all of them. It looked like a hundred, although I recalled that he said there were ten of them. I thought he'd been counting himself in that number.

Meeting the eyes of the men and women—the women were fiercer at first glance—I revised my previous opinion.

A den of hungry lions.

Every one of them, men and women, were lean, pale, and their features were striking. They had dark eyes, intense like Collum's. Was that a family trait? How did that even happen?

"Thank you for taking the time to welcome my guest," Collum said smoothly. "As I wasn't sure of your plans, I appreciate it." He inclined his head.

"It is our pleasure," a tall, dark-haired woman said. She was beautiful. They all were. "Is everything all right?" She looked at me then and then back at Collum.

"A man has come looking for me, and he contacted Isabeau," Collum said. "I find it concerning that someone would attempt such through an acquaintance."

"That is not normal," one of the men said. "You are right to be concerned.",

"My thoughts as well," Collum said, and there was an angry undertone to his words.

There was tension in the room, and it felt like it was more than just the concern for me and my safety. One of the women, who had blond hair and leaned against a tall man, nodded slightly.

"Let me show you to your room," Collum said. "There's a sitting room right next door, if you'd like to read, or are not ready for bed."

I inhaled deeply. "I don't know that I'll be good company tonight."

"Understandable," Collum said, his voice throttled down from only a moment before. "I'll come up and see that you have everything you need." He smiled, and I forgot everything—the den of lions, the frightening man earlier, the fact that he'd not called or contacted me in two days; it was all gone. His smile warmed me, and I found myself smiling back. Being close to him made all the negatives melt away.

When I looked around, I sensed amusement and pleasure from his cousins.

"There will be time for formal introductions later," Collum said, taking my arm, and carrying my luggage in the other hand.

I smiled at all the people still standing, standing so still, and let Collum lead me away. We walked up a wide flight of wooden stairs that had a landing partway up. The wood was old and dark and gleamed even in the low light. The stone walls looked warm and inviting, and I felt a sense of security that I'd been missing since Fergus approached me over dinner.

The stairs continued up, but Collum brought me down a hall that I thought went the length of the house. He stopped at a room that was next to the room on the end.

"This is your room," he said, opening the door. Inside, the walls were draped in ivory silk that billowed with the breeze from opening the door. The lights were low, almost like candlelight, and the room felt inviting.

"There's a bathroom over there." Collum pointed to the right. "And the sitting room is on the other side." He gestured to a door on the opposite side of the bathroom along the wall to the left. There was a dressing table in between the doors, and the bed was on the wall on the right, a tall four-poster draped with the same billowing fabric that adorned the walls.

"My room is at the end of the hallway," he added. "In case you need anything."

"I think I might take a bath and go to bed," I said. "I didn't think I was that tired, but all of a sudden, I'm exhausted." I felt safe, too. Given the fact that Fergus had robbed me of my sense of security for a time, I was grateful. "Thank you for offering your home to me."

"I'm glad to have you here," Collum said, taking my hand.

"We haven't talked in two days," I said, blowing my determination to not say anything. It made me feel needy, like a clingy girl. I didn't want that.

"No, we have not, and I am sorry. It was unavoidable," Collum said. He looked remorseful. It looked real.

I shrugged, trying to find a less needy vantage point for myself. "It's okay."

"No, it is not. It's not polite, and that is not normally like me. I'd like to make sure you're all right before you retire," he said.

I noticed that, at times, he got really formal. "Okay," I said.

Collum reached over and took my hand. He lifted it to his mouth and kissed the top of it. "Thank you for trusting me," he said.

I didn't reply, and he left, closing the door behind him. I did trust him, although I had no concrete reason to do so.

Oh, shit. I remembered the rest of my life abruptly. I'd need to let my parents know I'd switched hotels. Well, did I really? We talked over cell—they wouldn't know I'd gone to stay with someone I'd met three days ago.

I decided to call Gran tonight and let her know I'd gone through Dervaig.

As I was telling her, she gasped. "You did? How was it?"

"Gran, why didn't you come with me?"

"Because I'm too old and crotchety to travel. No one would have a good time, not even me. Besides, you've been sending me pictures, which I appreciate. How was Dervaig?"

I told her about the Bellachroy Hotel, which had been around since before Elizabeth's time.

"You think she was in there?"

"I think some of the trial might have been there, but the woman I talked with didn't know much of the history. I gave her my name and number so that the owner, or one of the former owners, or something"—I waved a hand even though I knew she couldn't see me—"could give me a call. There's not a lot there, Gran, even now. Apparently a lot of the village that is there now was built in the 1700s, except for the inn. It's the oldest inn on the island."

"I haven't seen any pictures from that," Gran scolded.

"It's been kind of busy," I said.

"Good! I'm glad to hear it. How are you enjoying Mull?"

"Gran, it's beautiful," I said honestly, the issues of the day momentarily forgotten. "And you weren't kidding in telling me to watch the driving video."

She laughed. "Please tell me you didn't hit any cows!"

"No, but it was close once. Although I think it was my fault because I was looking out the window."

We laughed together and talked some more. Finally, Gran

said, "I'm going to let you go to bed, You sound cheerful, but tired."

"I am. But I'm glad to talk to you."

"I love you, sweetheart," she said.

"I love you, too," I said. "And Gran?"

"Yes?"

"Thank you."

"You are so welcome, my Isa," she said.

I felt better after I hung up. Gran was happy knowing this was good for me, this was helping, and I was safe. I didn't know how I knew this, but I knew it. Collum would keep me safe.

With that comforting thought, I went to explore the bathroom, and draw a bath.

CHAPTER TWELVE

COLLUM

I strode downstairs, more pleased than I'd been in longer than I could remember to have Isabeau in my home. I could feel the rest of my coven waiting for me. The hum of their thoughts moved around mine.

Opening the door to the main floor study, they all turned. The nine people who had been my world and my focus for nearly two hundred years. Until now. Now that number had grown to ten.

"Why is he contacting her?" I asked. "Who is he? Why is he using Isabeau?"

"Who is this woman to you?" Margaret said. "I have heard a heart in the last week that I thought was a passing human. Just the hint of a heartbeat, one or two. When you came in with her, I heard two hearts." She gave me an intense stare.

I sighed. "When I met Isabeau three nights ago, my heart beat."

"It did?" Morag, the only other unmated vampire in our coven, asked. For the last hundred years or so, the rest of our coven had finally accepted that Morag and I were never going to be a couple. Prior to that, they'd had some hope.

Morag had never met anyone that she wanted to mate, either. We'd talked and determined that unless we got out in the human world more, we'd probably not come across a potential mate. She didn't seem all that bothered. I knew most of the vampires in the British Isles either personally or by sight. None had rung my bell, as it were. Not like Sarah, and not like Isabeau.

"It did," I said. "It has not been the same as before. With Sarah"—her name didn't hurt as much to say anymore—"my heart beat in quarter time with hers. With Isabeau, it's more random."

"Is that how you knew she was in danger?" Talbot asked.

"I could feel her fear," I said. That was new as well.

"That is interesting," Angus said.

"It is. But we can discuss that later. That's not the important factor at the moment."

"Does she know?" Clara asked.

"No. She does not. I have no plans to tell her at this point in time," I said harshly. "That's not the important factor, either."

Margaret made a noise that sounded very much like a snort, but she didn't say anything. That meant I'd hear from her later.

"What's important is who is Fergus MacDonald, or Fergus Mac, as he told Isabeau, and why is he after me? Why go through Isabeau?"

"You are foolish if you really think you must ask why," Devon, Margaret's mate, said. "That's not even a question."

I glared, but I didn't respond. I must have given myself away to a vampire who knew the signs of a bonded male. Even if it was only to myself, I was admitting I was bonded. But MacDonald must have been able to tell that. Which wasn't good. "Who is he? What have we found?" I asked.

"I contacted the registry in Edinburgh," Charlotte said.

"They have a listing for a Fergus MacDonald. He was already a several hundred years-old vampire at the time you were turned, Collum. He turned a human without permission, and the council issued a warrant for him. He disappeared." She looked down, biting her lip.

"What? Do not hold back," I said.

"While the council was never able to catch him and administer justice, he is suspected of staying in the area." She stopped again.

"What? Just say it!" I ran my hands through my hair in frustration.

"There were a number of vampires created after he disappeared. It continued for nearly twenty years—people would disappear and then there would be sightings."

"Like many of our sires." I looked around. Only Margaret knew her sire. The rest of us, myself included, had been made and left. Not all of us were from this area, and I was one of the older vampires in our coven. "Do we think he is the same as this Fergus in the records?"

"The bigger question is why he is hunting you?" Lyall mused.

"That is, indeed, the bigger question. The fact that he tracked me to Isabeau is concerning. It means he's here, watching." A thought struck me. "Three nights ago, I scented a vampire and human that were in the woods. I gave chase but lost them near Tobermory. That's when I met— Well, it doesn't matter. But that might have been MacDonald."

"It must be him," Clara said. "Any of our kind know that this is the MacLean coven's land, and do not just stroll onto the island without visiting their hosts."

"True," Angus said. "We need to assume that he is up to nothing good." The words sounded formal. Angus had never quite gotten the hang of modern speech.

"But why? Putting aside the interesting discussion of why he was here long ago, why is he here now, seeking me out?"

"You were right to bring her," Margaret said. "He would kill her. Which would be bad for you."

"What do you mean?"

She gave me a look that could have melted stone. "Because your heart beats for her."

"It's not like it was before," I said. I was hoping not to get into a discussion about my heartbeat at this very instant.

"That means nothing." Margaret waved my objections away. "Each mate is going to be different." Her lips curved into a smile. "Or did you expect that any woman would be the same as the last?"

My entire coven laughed softly.

I smiled. "No, I didn't make the mistake of making such an assumption. But—"

"There is no but. Your heart beats for her. She is your mate. The question is what will you do about it?"

"Nothing," I said. "I will do nothing."

Talbot and Devon laughed outright.

"All right, fearless leader. Please do nothing and see where that lands you." Margaret rolled her eyes.

"May we please focus on the matter at hand?"

"We are." Clara grinned at me.

"The other vampire, please," I ground out.

"We are, but that doesn't mean we're going to forget your human matter." Charlotte laughed as she spoke.

"That's fine. I don't even know what is going to happen with my human matter." I raised my voice to drown out the disbelieving comments. "I don't care why MacDonald is here, or what he wants. He's here, on our island. And that, we are not going to allow."

Now all them were nodding.

"Go out in teams of two. Morag, you're staying here with me. I want him found tonight."

"You should stay with her," Morag said. She was quiet and not given to grand speeches. Nor did she insist on being heard. "She's scared. I could smell her fear when she came in."

"I think she called you a den of lions."

"Well, she's no laggard, your human," said Devon. "She's aware of what is around her."

"Stay with her," Morag said again. "Once everyone leaves, he may see that as his chance. I will protect you, but it's better if you're with her."

"You will need help," I said.

She looked at me. "No, I shall not. Even if I did, your mind will be with the human, just as your heart already is. It is better for all if us if you stop denying the inevitable and go to her. Be with her so that you ascertain the health of your mate. I will protect you," she said once more, and I saw the savage in her behind her calm facade.

"All right. You're right, much as I hate to admit it."

"You'd rather be with her anyway," said Lyall. "We all understand. No one is feeling put out, or put upon, or anything other than empathetic and concerned for her health. We all know," he added seriously, all teasing gone, "that she must survive, one way or the other. You cannot lose another mate."

His mate, Clara, dug an elbow into his ribs so fast I almost didn't see it. Lyall leaned to the side slightly. "See what you miss? This is, of course, bliss."

Everyone laughed. Vampires weren't given to laughter, and many who lived together as a coven became intolerant and unkind. It was why many vampires didn't stay with their sires more than fifty years or so. The contempt grew too strong.

But we had all chosen one another. We were not bound by blood, as many covens were. We were bound by caring, and concern, and the desire to live together as family. I hadn't seen any of the petty squabbling that I'd seen in the last coven I nested with. Even as much as I had liked Serina and Thomas, and I loved Miles as a brother—he and I still communicated— that coven had disbanded by choice.

My entire being thrilled at the thought of spending the evening with Isabeau. I'd have to tell her something—she already knew there was something different about us. Oh, she hadn't figured it out, or gotten to the place where she was asking questions, but she knew. She knew merely from meeting me.

My Isabeau was a smart woman.

"All right. We are decided. We will go to him tonight, and bring him here, if you can. Tell him I promise to meet with him. But kill him if he will not come peacefully."

Margaret's brows lowered. I could feel her disapproval from where she stood. "Are you sure that is the best idea? We—you —will have to answer for such an action."

"He is on my land. He is seeking me out through humans. He is stalking my home, and he is working with a human. Where in that is a fellow vampire, wanting to work out what- ever difference or injury he feels has been done to him?"

She shrugged.

"I shall explain to the council if necessary. I have a feeling if he's lingering with humans, he has long been off their radar. He never answered for his crime all those years ago. If there is one thing the council excels at, it's holding a grudge, along with a long memory."

"That is true. All right, Collum. I shall help you and your human. For she is part of this whether she or you wish it." Margaret turned, and her mate followed her.

The rest filed out after them. Morag stayed with me. "I wish you had sent me out to scout. You know I'm the best."

"Yes, and you're the fiercest fighter, alongside Margaret. None of us are slackers, but you were right. Isabeau will be a problem for me, should he get here. I want the fiercest in the coven guarding us both."

A smile tipped the corners of Morag's mouth. She walked toward the door, touching my arm as she did. "It's not the eighteenth century anymore, Collum. We are far better prepared now."

I didn't reply as she left the room, leaving me to my own thoughts. Her last statement could apply to a lot of things. Now I needed to go and see to Isabeau. Exactly what I was supposed to see to, I had no idea.

But the thought of being with her was appealing. Very appealing.

I moved upstairs, not bothering to hide how I moved or how fast it was—I was home, and everyone here was the same. Except Isabeau.

And that was the problem, wasn't it? She wasn't like me, wasn't the same.

I knocked on the door.

"Come in," I heard her say. As I opened the door, I could smell the soap she'd used for the bath. The entire room had a warm feel, and it made Isabeau smell even better.

Holy Mary mother of God and all his angels, I thought. Give me strength.

CHAPTER THIRTEEN

ISABEAU

I looked up to see Collum come in. He stopped for a brief moment, his eyes closed and his face turned up— to what?

It was weird. Then he looked down and smiled at me. "You've had a bath. How do you feel?"

Even though his words were calm and smooth as any he'd ever spoken at me, there was something different about him. He was coiled and tense, although very good at hiding it.

"I did. The tub is like a pool. I enjoyed it, thank you." I tried not to gush. This was the guy who had just ghosted me after laying the best kiss of my life on me. I felt a pang for Jonathan. He might not have kissed me with the same intensity Collum did, but at least Jonathan called back. I shot a glare at Collum. *Not like you*, I thought.

His eyebrows went up as though he'd read my thoughts. "Are you all right?"

"Now that the moment of panic has passed, I'd like to talk to you."

The wariness around Collum increased. "Of course. May I sit down?"

I nodded, and he sat in a low chair across the small loveseat I was curled up on.

"What would you like to speak about?"

"Why didn't you call me?" I got straight to the point.

He hadn't expected that. "There are reasons—" He stopped. Then said, "It's not simple, Isabeau—" and stopped again.

I rolled my eyes as I crossed my arms, making sure he saw it. "Look, Collum, if you didn't want to see me again, just tell me. I'm a big girl. There's no need for beating around the bush."

"That's not it at all," he said, one hand running through his hair in frustration. He got up, walking to the window.

"Then what is it?" I resisted the urge to follow him and wind my arms around his waist. That's what my traitorous body wanted to do, but my head was in charge here, so I didn't move.

"It's not something I can explain," he said, talking to the window.

"What? I'm not smart enough? I don't need to worry my pretty head? And why is your creepy friend bothering me looking for you?" I stood up, unable to sit still. "Or do I not need to worry about that, either? I can't stay here forever, Collum! I have other places to be, and I have a life that doesn't revolve around whatever you've got going on!" I waved a hand in his direction.

He turned to face me then, his expression tortured. "It's not even that simple, Isabeau."

The way he said my name, it was almost a caress, and my anger faltered for a moment. But only for a moment. "Then explain it to me, because I need to leave two days from now."

"Why?"

"Because I have a schedule, and places to go, things to see." I crossed my arms.

"You are free to leave whenever you need to, but I'd really prefer it if you stayed until—"

"Until what? That's how kidnappings happen!"

"Until we find MacDonald."

"What is that about?"

He shrugged. "I wish I knew. I mean that. I don't know why he came to you. I agree that he should have approached me if it was really me he wanted to see. The fact that he didn't, that he came to you, a hu— a person who I've only just met, is suspicious."

The chill of fear ran through me as I recalled Fergus' expression and his cold eyes and manner. "Why would he want to try to get to you through someone else?"

It was like watching someone closing the shutters of a house. His expression became closed and guarded. "I don't know."

"You're lying," I said. "Which makes you just as suspect as Fergus MacDonald."

Collum took two steps toward me. "I am nothing like MacDonald."

"Then prove it."

"How?" His frustration was obvious.

"Let me go, and leave me out of this, this, whatever it is." I gestured with one hand, not sure what 'this' was, but I didn't want any part of the creepy MacDonald guy. I wanted Collum, and I wanted him badly. But not whatever he was mixed up in.

"I can't! If I could, I'd escort you off the island myself. But I can't!"

"What?" I felt his words like a blow to the chest. "Why?" I managed. I knew I had issues, but for God's sakes, they weren't bad enough for this kind of reaction. This outright rejection.

Collum took a few more steps, and he was right in front of me. How did he move so fast? Before I could think more about it, his arms were on my shoulders and his face near enough that I could feel his breath on my cheek.

"I can't let you go," Collum said. He practically growled the words.

"What?"

His lips captured mine, kissing me fiercely, devouring me, cutting off any further conversation.

I melted into him, not even thinking rationally. I wanted his hands, his lips, on me. Everywhere on me. I'd been dreaming of him since the moment I met him. It had been worse since our first kiss. His kiss now lived up to the memory. My body dissolved into a mixture of lust and need and want. My arms went around his neck.

With a groan, he brought me closer to him. I felt the hardness of him at my thighs, pressing against me.

I wanted him even closer. So close that no daylight existed between us. If he were more naked, that would be nice as well.

His lips trailed down my neck, and he inhaled deeply. "You smell wonderful," he breathed.

"Thank you?" What a strange thing to say, but whatever. I'd take it.

Just like the last time we'd kissed, Collum pulled away. "I'm so sorry, Isabeau. I shouldn't have done that." He sounded far older than twenty-six.

"Shut up," I said, reaching for him, and bringing him back to me. "I'm not. Shut up and kiss me again."

"I can't," he protested.

"Oh, yes you can. And you're not leaving me hanging again!"

"What do you mean?"

I glared. Then realization hit.

"Oh," he said. His eyes moved over me in a predatory fashion, leaving me feeling exposed.

I loved it. With this man, I loved it. I wanted more, not less, exposure.

Without waiting on him to rationalize his way out of this, I reached for him, and this time, it was my lips seeking his. His arms went around my waist and pulled me closer. One hand went down to my ass, to squeeze it. His other hand tangled in my hair, holding me as he kissed me, his hesitation apparently forgotten. Or at least shelved for the time being.

I'd take it.

Without letting go of me, he moved me toward the bed. I let him, because I was more than willing to go there. When my knees hit the bed, I sank down, taking him with me.

Collum pulled away. Why the hell did he keep doing that?

"I need to go and get something," he said. "If you're sure."

"I have never been surer," I responded.

He smiled, his eyes warming as he looked at me, even as I could see the hunger in him. Then he all but zoomed out of the room and was back while I was wondering how he moved so damn fast. It was a question I'd need to ask him—later.

I looked at what he held in his hands. "An entire box?"

"Call me optimistic," he said, his mouth widening in a grin.

I laughed. "What are you waiting for, then?" I asked as I scooted myself up the bed. "Don't just stand there."

"I like looking at you."

"Oh," I said. His gaze, as it had been since the moment I'd met him, was intense, and it made me want to turn away. But I didn't. I held it and watched the emotions that moved through his eyes.

It was intoxicating.

Collum set the box down and crawled onto the bed over top of me. Nudging my legs apart, he settled himself in between them. "I shouldn't be doing this," he murmured, holding my face in his hands, and kissing me between his words. "But I cannot resist you."

"Good," I said.

He kissed down the side of my neck, nipping me a little. His teeth were sharp, and I gasped.

"I'm sorry," I heard him say.

"My, what big teeth you have," I drawled. It had hurt, but that didn't mean I wanted him to stop.

I felt his chuckle next to my breast. Then he pushed my t-shirt up, and his mouth sucked at the nipple. Again, I felt a brush of pain as one of his teeth scraped against me, and it made my panties wet as I arched against him. Who knew teeth could be so fucking amazing?

He slid to the other breast, sucking at the nipple and his hand drifted down to my pajama bottoms. His fingers were cool against my belly, and they slipped between me and the waistband. He moved a little to give himself more access to me, a move I heartily approved of.

I hadn't felt so alive in… in a long time.

Slowly, achingly slowly, his fingers reached between my legs, and pushed into me. I gasped, unable to keep quiet.

Collum's mouth was next to mine. He kissed me tenderly, his finger, and then fingers, moving in and out of me. His thumb caressed my clit, and I moaned.

"You are so beautiful," he said against my mouth. "I need to taste you."

Then his mouth was gone from mine, and his fingers slid out of my pajamas. Before I could say a word, he was sliding my PJs down, tossing them to the floor. He moved between my legs, and I felt his breath against my thigh.

It was erotic. He spread my legs, and dipped his tongue into my cleft, and I forgot everything else. My head rolled to the side, and I moaned.

He was really, seriously, amazingly good at this.

I jumped as he took my clit in his mouth. He sucked at it, and then I felt a small prick of his teeth.

My orgasm, which had not seemed that close, happened almost instantly, and I cried out, "Oh, my God!"

He didn't stop, his mouth was still on me, pushing me and not letting me go—and I came again.

His fingers slid into me, moving easily with the slickness he'd made happen. In and out, while he suckled my clit, and I couldn't keep still. His free hand held my thigh down on the bed, which was probably a good thing as I wanted to clench them together. I didn't want to kill him in the middle of sex.

That would suck.

"Oh, my, God," I gasped. "Oh, oh... Collum!" I felt myself orgasming again. What was this? The Marvelous Tongue and his Magical Clit act?

Not that I cared. My heart beat like a drum in my ears as I felt myself relax from Collum's ministrations.

"So, you liked it?" He stopped what he was doing to look up at me from between my legs.

CHAPTER FOURTEEN

COLLUM

Her mouth fell open. "Well, actually, now that you ask, no. It was all right, but your technique needs some work."

I started to retort when I realized she was teasing. This was the real Isabeau—this small, sassy glimpse gave me an idea of the life that had been taken from her when her friends had died.

I found I was just as pleased at giving her pleasure as I was to see her being herself.

"Well, I will happily take any suggestions under advisement," I said, sliding up her body, which felt right next to mine.

She felt right.

She tasted right.

I'd tasted blood from her nipple and her clit—not on purpose, but my instinct was to bite—and her blood made me want her like I'd wanted nothing in my life. My cock was hard, and it wanted her, too.

She was my mate.

There was no denying it. This was the woman I was meant to be with.

Isabeau laughed. "Good thing you're open to suggestion. I have one, if you'd like to hear it."

"I am all ears," I said.

"Get that box out."

I looked to the side of the bed and found where it had fallen to the floor. I tore open the box, taking out one, and then shed my clothing.

"You're beautiful," Isabeau said, all traces of laughter gone. Her voice was soft, almost reverent. "You are absolutely beautiful."

I opened the packet and rolled it on, watching her eyes watch me. It was a simple act, but her face as she watched me made it one of the seductive moments between us so far. Which was saying something.

Part of me cursed myself. I shouldn't be doing this. This would only make everything more difficult—but I couldn't stop myself.

I didn't want to.

Isabeau's arms came up to my neck, bringing me closer to her. I lay between her legs, allowing my cock to rest against her. My eyes held hers, and I knew myself lost.

Carefully, wanting to maintain control, I slid into her slowly. She was warm, so warm.

Isabeau gasped quietly.

"Are you all right?"

She nodded but didn't speak. Her legs twined around me, urging me on. I thrust into her, and... it was the best moment I'd had with another in hundreds of years. I had to blink, because my vision flashed. This must be what it meant when humans said they saw stars.

I saw stars with Isabeau.

Her back arched, bringing her chest closer to me, and I leaned down to take her nipple into my mouth. I could feel her nails scratch against my back as I drew back and plunged in again.

I pushed myself up onto my arms and met her gaze once more, and I drove into her, again and again. I could feel my control slipping and I struggled to maintain it. My fangs touched the edge of my lips. I'd been trying to keep them from her, but I wasn't sure I'd be able to.

Her eyes were on mine as I penetrated her. It felt as though we were trying to become one. I'd never bedded Sarah, although we'd been intimate—as intimate as she would allow. I had no experience of sleeping with the one you were meant for, although I'd been with any number of women over the centuries.

This was unlike any other woman I'd ever known.

Isabeau's breath was coming in small, panting gasps that matched the time of our movement, and I could feel myself getting close.

I didn't want this to end. I stopped.

"No," she whispered.

"Turn over," I whispered back.

Her eyes looked at me for a moment, uncomprehending.

I moved back, leaving her body.

She got it and rolled over to her stomach. Her ass lifted slightly, and the sight nearly drove me wild. I thrust back into her, and the difference of our joining was amazing. I pulled her closer to me, my hands gripping her hips and pounding into her.

Isabeau lifted herself up onto her hands and pushed herself against me. I hammered into her again and again, feeling myself getting closer to the climax. Never had I felt like this. Isabeau pushed up against me so that she was up on her knees in front of me, her back pressed against my chest. I wrapped an arm around her waist, and the other tangled in her hair, pulling her head back and exposing her neck.

My fangs jutted forward at the sight of her long, pale neck. The throb of her heartbeat right in front of me—the blood pulsing just beneath her skin—made me hold her to me, thrusting upward.

Isabeau was gasping each time I did, and my hands slipped a little with the sheen of sweat on her body. I licked the side of her neck, loving her taste.

"Oh, God, oh, Collum," she screamed, and I could feel her warmth surround me as she came.

I gave myself over to it—to her—then. One final lunge, and I found my release.

Her head lolled back onto my shoulder. My lips were at the base of her neck, and without thinking, I sank my teeth into her.

Isabeau's head snapped forward.

Shit.

Oh holy hell dear Mary mother of God I'd bitten her.

A spurt of blood filled my mouth.

Shit.

I swallowed, then bit my tongue and felt my own blood well up. Using my tongue, I licked at the bite marks I'd made on her neck. My blood would heal her and maybe help cover my fuck-up.

We stilled, and I felt her body relax. My own was still alive with sensation—I felt so much of what Isabeau was feeling, and it was nearly overwhelming, after so many years of keeping feelings at bay. It was a struggle not to bite her again.

"Oh, my," Isabeau said. "That was..."

"Yes. It was," I said. My voice was hoarse with need. The blood lust was almost overpowering. I wanted to drink from her, taste more of her, feel her response. But now was not the moment. I wanted it to be, but it wasn't the right time. Damn it all to hell.

I shifted, and we were no longer one. I felt a sense of loss.

Isabeau fell onto her hands and crawled up the bed to roll over and look at me.

"I didn't— Holy shit, Collum! What's going on with your teeth?" She scrabbled up to the head of the bed, pulling the blankets with her.

Shit. My fangs. I touched one with the tip of my tongue.

What in the name of hell and all the demons did I do now?

"You mean these?" I touched them again.

"Yes, I mean those! Is that what you've been biting me with?"

"Well, they do sometimes nip when I'm not planning on it," I said, trying to stay casual. I looked down. This was not the way to have this discussion. "Isabeau, I'm the same man you met."

Her head tilted as she looked at me with disbelief. "Um, I don't think I know who I met."

"Fair point. May I please go and clean up?" I held up my hands. "I'll tell you whatever you want to know, answer any question you have." I felt as though a bomb might go off if I wasn't careful. An Isabeau bomb.

A moment that stretched to an eternity, and then she nodded, the blankets still up around her chin.

I didn't bother trying to hide my speed. I hurried to the bathroom, cleaned myself up, and then came back out and pulled on my pants. I slowed then, sitting on the edge of the bed, keeping a distance between us. I didn't want her to run.

"Explain," Isabeau said.

I sighed. "I'm like you in that I was a human—"

"Was? What the hell does that mean?" She shrank from me, pressing herself against the headboard, and clutching the blankets like a drowning woman holding a life vest.

"It means that in 1483, when I was twenty-six, and in the middle of a battle between my laird and his son, I was bitten and changed by a vampire."

"They're real?" she whispered.

"We are. I died on that beach, the beach that is just north of Tobermory. I died, and then I woke, and I was alone, surrounded by the dead men of my family, and starving, and with no idea what had happened to me."

"I thought you guys lived together, or had internships, or something."

"Internships?" I laughed despite the seriousness of the moment.

A flush moved up her cheeks. "Hey, I'm just going off all the books about women falling in love with vampires."

"I haven't read those. Perhaps I should. It might make this easier," I sighed. "The point is, I'm not human anymore. I'm not alive, but I'm not dead. I can't go out during the day. I drink blood to stay alive—"

"You kill people?" Her voice came out as a whisper.

"Not anymore. That's another story, but no. Not anymore."

"Do most vampires?"

This was, understandably, a sticking point. "Yes."

"Why me?" she asked.

Trust her to get the heart of the question. "Because we were supposed to meet."

"I don't understand," Isabeau said. "And I don't know that I want to. No!" She held up a hand, stopping me from coming closer, letting the blankets fall off her shoulder. "I think I need you to leave."

"Isabeau, I'll go, but are you going to leave? I don't think you should. It's not safe until we catch MacDonald."

"Are all of you vampires?"

"Yes." I hated seeing the fear move across her face.

"I don't understand how this... I... I'm struggling here," Isabeau said. "Okay, I take it back. You need to stay. I'm not leaving either. But you are going to talk."

I reached a hand to her, and she stuck her hand at me

again, insisting that I stop coming toward her. I complied. Even though I couldn't countenance her leaving, and I couldn't bear to think of turning her. I didn't want to scare her away.

"I get it," I said.

"It explains a lot." She looked down at the blankets. Then back at me. "You're kind of old fashioned."

"I don't think that's a bad thing," I said, not wanting to laugh. I remembered that she was still young, only in her twenties, even if life had aged her far beyond that.

Isabeau inhaled deeply and exhaled. "Okay. I want you to tell me everything. Everything. How you turned into a vampire, your life, everything."

"Five hundred—" I stopped when I saw the expression on her face. "All right. I'll tell you."

And I started from the beginning, from the battle of my clan where I lost my human life, and the time after that where I struggled to learn to survive in this new body, finding the coven in London.

"You left them?"

"Vampires will nest together for a time, but we often split after a number of years."

"How long has your... your coven been here?"

"I bought this house in 1720. The family had died out, and it was up for auction. I was able to buy it, and over the last three hundred years I've brought all the members in." I debated sharing my desires about having family, and decided she had the right to hear it all. "I have always envied those of us who had blood ties—because I have no idea who my sire was. He or she left me on the beach to live or die on my own." My voice hardened. "I survived, but I've seen how close those tied by blood can be. I will never know that, and I didn't want to spend the rest of my existence alone. There have been a number of vampires in the Highlands who also did not know their sire, and the ones here are those I've met and enjoyed. We've all been together for about one hundred and fifty years, which is significant in our world."

"You're like a home for lost vampires."

I shrugged. "Some. They have to be people I can get along with, who fit in with those already here."

"Go on. I'm sure that more has happened since you bought this place to now."

I sighed, to give myself more time to consider my words. "There is. On the whole, it's been a quiet three hundred years, and I'm glad. I prefer the quiet."

"Why is that?"

I felt liquid well at the corner of my eye. Even now, it was difficult to speak of it.

CHAPTER FIFTEEN

Isabeau

Something in his face shifted, and then incredibly, a dark tear slid down his face.

"Is that blood?" I whispered. All of this was a major mind-blowing experience. In order to not run screaming from here—because one, I was naked, and two, I'd just had mind-blowing sex with this guy who was five hundred years old, a vampire, and who had bitten me—after the best sex I'd ever had--I focused on the story he was telling me. I could cry in the shower later. I hoped.

"Yes. I don't cry often, but when we do, it's blood."

"What is making you cry?"

He shifted on the bed, not looking at me, and then he met my eyes. "Before I moved back to Scotland, while I was living in London, I met a woman. A young woman, much like you. And... we fell in love. Eventually—although it wasn't that long when I looked back now—I shared my truth, as I'm doing with you."

"What did she say?"

His gaze went over my head, and I could tell that he was

seeing that time in the past. "She stroked my cheek and told me that she'd always known something was different with me. I asked her to join me, and she agreed." He smiled at the memory.

I found that a small stab of jealousy hit my heart. Which really wasn't the response I was hoping for here. All that he was telling me should be turning me away from him, sex aside. But it wasn't.

"I'd found her because my heart beat for the first time since I was made after I met her. Like it beat when I met you."

"Wait, what? Your heart beats because of me?"

"Our hearts stop when we are made. When we meet our mates"—his eyes never wavered from mine—"our hearts will begin to beat. They will beat as long as our mate, if she be human, is alive. But I've never known anyone who has met their mate twice in a lifetime. Most don't lose their mates the first time." His head dropped.

My head whirled again. This was like being drunk and trying to drive. You knew that you had to keep it together, or bad shit was about to happen—but it was almost too difficult.

"Wait, what are you saying?"

"I'm saying that when I met you in the cemetery, my heart started to beat. I didn't want to believe it. I've never heard of it, and after what happened to Sarah—" He stopped, putting his hand over his eyes and rubbing with his fingers.

"What happened to her?"

When Collum looked up, his face was bleak. All the angles and planes were sharper. "I drained her. That's what you do to make another vampire. I gave her some of my own blood when she was nearly gone. After that, you have to let the new one sleep, and then they will wake. But she never woke." His voice broke, and he looked away then. "I kept her with me for three days, hoping that she was just taking her time, that it was happening slowly. But she never woke. I killed her."

I covered my mouth with my hand, feeling tears spring to my eyes at the sound of his words; the pain that was like a physical thing. I didn't know what to say.

Collum continued. "When you meet your mate, and she is human, there are two choices, because there are some who have met their mates as vampires. But if she's human, you can either live with her for her human life, or you turn her, and you have eternity. I tried to bring Sarah with me, and I failed. When my heart beat at meeting you, I was not only astonished, but terrified. I've never attempted to make another vampire."

"Is that why you don't kill anyone when you're eating?" How I kept my voice steady with that sentence, I didn't know. *You survived an avalanche,* I told myself. *You can do this.*

He nodded, and I could feel the pleasure in my question coming off him. Which was weird as hell?

"I killed because I needed to. After Sarah, if I am very hungry, I will feed from more than one human. It's not easy, or at least, it wasn't then, but it's habit now."

"What about the rest of your family?" I asked. I remembered the feeling I'd had walking in here. Apparently, my sense of self-preservation was working, even if I hadn't realized it at the time.

"Some still kill, some do not. We do not hunt on the island. No child is ever to be harmed. I know of one who likes to prey on criminals, people who hurt their partners, children. My family is one that I'm proud of, Isabeau. They are good people still, even if we are all more vampire than anything else."

"I guess that's good," I said slowly. "I'm going to change the subject here. Why did you come in here, and why did we have sex?"

"I beg your pardon?" His eyebrows went up, and he completely retreated into formality.

"What's the goal here? So I'm your mate? Is that why I'm

drawn to you so strongly? Is that why I can't think straight around you? Why don't I get any say in this?"

He shrugged. "I don't know. I don't understand the reasons behind it. It doesn't happen for everyone. People are together because most of us don't want to be alone, but not all who are together are mated. It's considered lucky to find your mate. Do you not care for me?"

The question was asked casually, but it wasn't casual at all.

"I do, and I have been trying to figure out why I care so much. Now I know. It has nothing to do with me, or what I want."

"I'm going to disagree, having seen those who have found their mates. Those who are mated are good couples, a strong pair. They complement one another. I have always seen it as the vampire version of true love at first sight."

That made sense, although I wasn't ready to concede. "Okay, then what is the end goal?"

He looked at me blankly.

"What do you see happening?"

"We only have two choices. I am with you until you live out your human life, or you become one of us."

There it was, in stark black and white. "I'm just getting my life back, Collum," I said, whispering. The weight of what he'd said sat heavily on me. "I don't know that I want either of those choices. What happens if I leave?"

A flash of pain crossed his face. It was fleeting, but I saw it. "That is your choice, Isabeau. Just as it would be your choice to walk away from a man in the human world."

I nodded. "Okay, so there are three choices."

He nodded. "I suppose you are right."

"What do you want?" I asked.

"Me?"

I nodded.

Collum sighed. I hadn't seen him really do that before

tonight, and I wondered if he needed to breathe. But he'd smelled me, so maybe it was something he liked? I stopped my train of thought—I didn't need any distractions right now.

"I want you with me. I find you to be amazingly strong. You have suffered as I have—lost the thing you loved the most. That sort of pain changes you. And I appreciate that you know that change, even as I am sorry you've had to experience it. But it makes you more like me, and I like that, selfish as that may sound." His lips thinned as he stopped, and then he spoke again. "I am reluctant to try to turn you. I would not take your life from you. I don't know why Sarah never woke. I've tortured myself, wondering if it was me, if I did something incorrectly. I don't know, and I won't risk you. So that means that I would like you to stay with me for your lifetime, then."

"Even when I am old and wrinkly?"

"That doesn't matter. You will always be you."

"I don't know if I want to be a vampire," I said, getting the words out before I lost my nerve. "This has been a tough year for me. I don't like the idea of giving up my life to something I have no say in."

Collum opened his mouth, then closed it.

"What?"

"Does the thought of being with me not please you?"

"Are you kidding me? You were here fifteen minutes ago. That's the best sex I've ever had. I don't think it's because you're just a Mr. Wizard in the sack, either. I think it's because we're connected."

His face underwent a few transformations. "I think that was a compliment."

"It was. Don't get all big-headed about it. Is that part of the whole mate thing?"

"Is sex not better with the one you love?"

"You love me?" I ask.

"I will," he said.

That silenced me. Something—some vampire thing? Something else?—had brought us together and put the heavy vibes on both of us; I guess to make sure we didn't miss it? But I didn't really know him, even as I'd gotten the summary of his life. That wasn't knowing a person.

But didn't I? He'd asked me to come and stay, and I'd agreed with no hesitation, because being with him made me feel safe. We'd fallen into bed pretty quickly, and my thoughts hadn't been worried. No, they'd been all 'Hell, yeah!'

So maybe the soul piece of me knew him. Maybe that was it. Our souls recognized each other, and the people we were needed more time.

I found I liked that explanation better than anything I'd heard so far.

"Isabeau?" Collum asked.

"Sorry. I was thinking."

"Yes?" His tone was inviting.

I shook my head. "I need you to leave now. I appreciate that you've been so open, but I need to think about all this."

He got up without saying anything. He picked up his clothing and moved toward the door. Then he stopped and came around the side of the bed to stand near me.

I held myself very still. He leaned down and kissed me gently.

"Tonight was incredible for me, Isabeau. I need you to know that."

I looked up at him. After five hundred years, he must have had some pretty amazing nights.

"It was. You are unique. I will not see you until tomorrow evening. May I ask that you stay here, so that I know you are safe?"

Oh, shit. I'd forgotten about Fergus MacCreepy for a moment. I nodded.

"Thank you. I have help that is here during the day. Ned,

and his wife, Constance. They know what we are, and they will get you anything you need. I'll let them know you're here. They'll be pleased," he said, his face relaxing for a moment. "It's been a while since we've had a human here."

"Okay," I said.

"Good night, Isabeau." Without another word, he walked to the door, not moving as fast as he'd moved before. He turned to smile at me and then closed the door gently behind him.

I slumped against the headboard.

Holy shit. What had I fallen into? For no reason that I could easily discern, I felt the tears start down my face.

CHAPTER SIXTEEN

COLLUM

I went to my room. Ever since we'd slept together, my heart had been beating more regularly. My head, my senses—they were all full of Isabeau. I'd tried to keep all the explanations as simple as possible.

She was amazing. I hadn't been lying, or even stretching the truth, when I told her that our time tonight had been fantastic. I'd never felt so on the verge of losing control, of wanting to give so much, of wanting to be so close to another.

If anything, I'd spent a lot of time keeping boundaries in place. I didn't ever want to hurt like I had with Sarah again.

But Isabeau gave me something different. She wasn't better or worse than Sarah—she was different.

I couldn't tell how we'd left things. I appreciated her honesty, even as it filled me with dread. I hadn't thought of her third choice—that she would choose to ignore our bond.

I shook my head. I couldn't think of that. I went to my bathroom and showered. My clan would know we'd been together, but the scent of her, of what we'd done—I didn't want it on public display.

Once I'd cleaned up, I sought out Morag. "Anything new?" I asked.

She looked at me with a smile. "Other than you finally got laid? No. No sign of MacDonald. The rest aren't back yet."

I smiled back. "I don't know if I'm up for discussing that quite yet, but yes, I did. And I wish they'd come back, or he'd show up, or something." I flexed my fingers, trying to work off the energy that surged through me.

"Take a run around the place," Morag said. "It's like standing next to live energy." She rubbed her arms. "You're making *me* twitchy."

"You'll take care of her?"

"Of course, Collum." Morag's eyes softened. "With my life."

"Thank you," I said. Then I ran from the house. Morag was right. I needed to be outside, doing something. I ran in the night, inhaling the cool scents of the evening, on the hunt for anyone who didn't belong on my land.

But there was no one. The rest of my coven was either hunting MacDonald, or hunting for themselves, which meant they wouldn't be back until just before dawning, if they returned this evening. We had a system where those who didn't plan to return would text. While there were things about the modern world I wasn't fond of—I missed corsets on women, and men's clothing was looser and more comfortable during my time—the cell phone was a marvelous thing. It took a great deal of worry and concern for one's coven out of the equation.

I ran with a feeling of joy I'd not felt for years, and as I ran, I could find no trace of anyone who might mean us harm.

Which made me nervous.

When I returned to the house, Morag was reading. She looked up. "Your Isabeau hasn't stirred. Other than to take a shower, I think. The water pipes were making all sorts of racket."

"Thank you," I said.

"No, thank you. You feel better." Morag spoke with authority. "Did you find anything?"

"No, and that worries me. Why did he approach her and then leave?"

"The might and fearsome strength of your amazing coven?" Morag regarded me with a great deal less concern than I felt.

"I don't think so, mighty and fearsome though you are." I smiled at her despite my worry.

"It makes no sense. I agree with you there. But there is nothing we can do outside of what we're doing. We either catch him and rend him to pieces, or we wait for him to come here and do the same. We don't have many options until he shows himself, Collum. And we will keep your human safe. Did you tell her?" She changed the subject abruptly.

"Weren't you listening?" I asked wryly.

"You know, I do try to give all of my coven mates privacy. It's difficult, as you know." She gave me what she called the 'hairy eyeball' look. "Because the rest of them are so noisy. But I try. So no, I wasn't listening."

As the only two members of our coven who weren't mated, I understood her reference. Sometimes it was difficult with the mated members of our family. Having just spent an amazing time with Isabeau, I also understood the noise factor. I smiled. "I told her because my fangs popped out at a rather unfortunate moment."

Morag looked at me and then burst out laughing. "Collum, the possibilities behind your calm statement are just endless!" She let out peals of laughter.

I rolled my eyes. Morag was one of the youngest of us and lacked some of the heavier formality the older members, me included, had. It was one of the reasons I'd asked her to join us. I liked her immensely. The rest of the coven thought that meant that I'd found a mate, but for me, it was more like a younger sister. I'd been older than my siblings and hadn't had the time to enjoy having them when I was human. Morag made us all laugh at ourselves.

"Do you need to hunt?"

She shook her head. "No. I will tomorrow, but if you'd like to go and stew in your rooms, I am content to keep watch. What did she say?"

Perhaps she was a little too informal, I thought, feeling the sting of her words. However, she wasn't wrong. But I focused on her question. "She was... taken aback," I said.

Morag laughed even harder.

I waited for her to finish.

"So she wasn't bowled over at the thought?"

"Oh, I think she was bowled over, but I'm not sure it did my case any good," I said, crossing my arms.

"And that is what is making you crazy," Morag said.

"It is." I'd learned long ago not to bother denying things with Morag. "It's never been like this, Morag. Not even... not even before."

"Kind of sucks having to put yourself out there," Morag said, no trace of laughter in her words. "I get it. It's even harder for you, crazed Highlander manly man." She shook her head. "And you all wonder why I'm not keen to find a mate. An occasional partner is just fine for me. Far less trouble."

Now it was my turn to laugh. "You sound like a man, Morag."

She shrugged. "Okay, sexist pig. No, no, don't get all in a bunch. I know you can't help it, being a thousand years old. I just don't see the point. I love my life. I love being a vampire. Who needs love to make a muddle of things?"

"Who, indeed?"

"That wasn't permission for you to start sulking. Stop it," she said. "If you recall, none of our coven came by their love easily. Another mark against it," she added. "So consider this some of the work for your reward."

"She asked what happens if one of the people just walks away," I said quietly.

Morag turned to me, all joking gone. "She did?"

I nodded.

"Oh, shit."

I nodded again. I'd never met anyone who turned from their bonded mate. It just wasn't done. More so, I didn't know what I would do if she walked away.

"I'm sorry," Morag said. "I mean that, too."

"I know."

She got up, stretching. Then she came and put her arm around my waist, leaning against me. I liked the closeness. This was the reason I'd spent so much time creating a family, even without the ties of blood. I put my arm around her shoulders.

"It will work out," she said.

"I hope so," I said. "I don't like not knowing."

"If she wants to be with you, it must be of her own free will."

"I know that. But—"

"You expected her to be overjoyed."

"Well, perhaps."

"Give her time. She hasn't run screaming from the house, so that's a good sign."

I bade her goodnight and returned to my quarters to spend most of the night pacing, wondering what Isabeau was doing.

I wanted to go next door and talk to her, see where her thoughts were. But even with my limited experience with women, I knew that wouldn't be a good call. I didn't need Morag to tell me that.

During the night, I heard from the rest of the coven. They had fanned out in teams of two and were tracking MacDonald. Angus and Kyla were tracking the human who had separated from MacDonald. So he was working with a human—was this the human and vampire I'd scented on my lands? What was he doing? Something about this tugged at the corner of my brain but after the evening I'd had, I was too tired to puzzle it out.

I found that I was relieved for the dawning—I wanted to sleep and then wake to tackle all the things that had come up today with fresh eyes, with eyes not blinded by Isabeau.

I didn't know if that was possible, however. I'd been so keen on not making her aware of what fate had in store for us. Now, not only had I told her everything, but I'd been intimate with her.

I didn't know how I would be able to let her go.

CHAPTER SEVENTEEN

ISABEAU

After a long shower and a retreat to bed where I fell asleep with tears rolling down my cheeks, I woke to see the sunlight peeking around the edges of the long curtains in front of the window on the other end of the room.

What the hell had I gotten myself into? I nearly fell out of the bed when the door opened and an older woman came bustling in.

"Miss Isabeau, I'm here to let you know that breakfast is ready. You can join us down the stairs, or I can bring you up a tray."

"I'm... I'm sorry, who are you?" I asked.

"I'm Constance, and I'm here to help you with anything you need," she said, stopping to smile broadly at me. "Collum let us know he had a guest last night. Are you hungry, dearie?"

I remembered that Collum told me he had people here in the daytime. It made sense.

"Um, yes."

"You want me to bring you up something?" she asked, opening the curtain.

"No, no, I'll get up. Where is breakfast? The kitchen?"

Constance nodded.

"Thanks for letting me know. I'll get dressed and be down shortly."

"Take your time. I'll keep it warm for you." With another smile, she bustled out.

That had been unexpected. But I found that, despite all that had happened, I was hungry. I got up and made myself presentable and went downstairs.

I had no idea where the kitchen was. But this was an old house, so maybe at the back? I moved down the hall and the smell of bacon told me I was on the right path. The hallway opened up to a large, sunny kitchen done in stone and white and yellow. There was a large wooden table in the middle where Constance was leaning over, and an older man sat across from where she stood.

"Well, good morning, Miss Isabeau!" She beamed at me. "Have a seat." She indicated a chair to the right of the man. "That's Ned, my husband. We take care of Lochdon House."

"Good morning." Ned smiled. His voice was softer than that of his wife's. "And welcome."

"Thank you." I eased into the chair. I found I was a little sore all over, as though I'd had a tough workout the day before.

Well, I kind of had. I ducked my head down to hide my grin, not wanting to explain anything. I could tell I was giggly because I was on the edge of...something. I didn't know what. Nothing seemed quite real. Everything Collum told me the night before was still rattling around in my brain.

It made sense, but... it didn't. I think what I was grappling with—

"I'm sorry?" I asked. I realized that Constance and Ned were looking at me.

"I asked what brings you to Mull? You sound American," Constance said.

"Oh, I'm sorry. I was woolgathering. I'm looking up family records."

"Oh, you're from here?"

"Well, an ancestor of mine was."

"Really? Who?"

"Her name was Elizabeth Martin. She was from Dervaig, in the sixteen hundreds," I added.

"Are your family still here?" Ned asked.

"Not as far as I know. From what my gran told me, Elizabeth was tried as a witch."

Both Constance and Ned stopped what they were doing and looked at me, eyebrows raised.

"Well, that would explain why your family might have left the island," Constance said. "People were right mad about what they considered witchcraft. Mostly old women," she added with a sniff.

"Not that we're ones to say anything. We work with vampires," Ned said.

"You know?" I asked before I could help myself, even though Collum had mentioned it.

Constance laughed, and Ned grinned.

"Of course, we do. Collum was honest with us. He's been good to us. Ned was hurt at work, and we didn't know what we were to do. Collum came to see us one evening and made us the offer of care-taking. We hire help as needed, and all is good." She beamed.

"He's a good man," Ned added.

"You're okay with the whole vampire thing?" I asked. This was surreal.

"Well, I won't deny it was a bit of a shock," Constance said. "I'd thought they were just a story, you know? But there's lots I don't know. And now that I do, I like all the family that lives here. They care about this place."

Ned asked me where I'd been, and the talk moved to the more mundane, thankfully.

After breakfast, I went back to my room, and got showered and went outside. The house was high on a hill. It was surrounded by trees, and there didn't seem to be any neighbors. I could see down to the water from where we were, and as I hiked around the back of the house and through the woods, there was a small lake.

It was idyllic.

I headed back to the house as the sun was reaching the middle of the sky overhead, and Ned was coming out of the side door. "There's lunch in the kitchen, if you're inclined," he said as he passed.

I nodded and made my way back to the kitchen. Unlike this morning, Constance had things to do, because she showed me where she'd put out some sandwiches, and then left me on my own.

I was glad. I had a lot to think about. As I ate, I allowed myself to consider what Collum had told me. I could either live with him as a human or vampire, or I could leave. It had been interesting to me that the last choice was not one on his list. When I'd mentioned it, he'd been surprised.

Maybe because no one ever turned away from a mate? I didn't know.

But I didn't like the idea that my fate was decided for me based on reasons I didn't know, much less understand.

I'd spent a year in limbo, hiding from everything. This trip had me feeling alive for the first time since I'd lost the people I loved most. I felt like I was finding myself again.

And because I was really attracted to a guy, all of a sudden, we were soul mates, and I was tied to him forever?

Collum seemed to accept this as a fact, and I supposed it was due to knowing people—vampires—who had made a life with their mate.

I found this a struggle to take in. Rather than stew the rest of the day, I spent it going around the house, taking the time to look over the art, and the books, and all the things that reeked of history. I loved this house. It was completely different from what I knew. The house felt like the rest of the island—solid, permanent, and at ease with the past.

It was me who couldn't come to terms with my past.

That was the thing, wasn't it? I sighed, leaning my head back to let the sun warm my face. I couldn't face a future of forever when I struggled with my past.

I knew I'd have to speak with Collum tonight, and while part of me wanted more of the lovely, delicious sex please, that wouldn't be possible in any realm if we didn't talk. As the evening grew closer, I found it impossible to sit still, or to settle. Finally, I made my way to my room. I didn't know if the rest of the vampires were here, and I wasn't having this conversation out in public.

But didn't vampires have amazing hearing? I wondered how much of the urban legends were true. I knew they moved fast. Watching Collum move was amazing.

The moment the sun disappeared behind the mountain I heard a knock on my door. With my heart in my throat, I called out, "Come in."

Collum came through the door. Damn it all, he was beautiful. His expression was guarded, although he was pleased to see me. He came right to me and put his arms around me. "I am glad to see you," he said.

As though they had a mind of their own, my arms came up and wrapped around his waist. He felt good. He smelled good. I could feel myself relaxing into him. The nerves of earlier today were easing into the distance. Just being near him made me feel better.

Was this the mating thing?

No wonder it worked well for the people who were caught

up in it. This was like a drug. At that moment, there was nowhere else in the entire world I'd rather be.

Wait, wait. No. Reluctantly, my entire being screaming at moving away from him, I let go of him and took a step back. When I looked up, he was smiling at me.

"How was your day? Constance and Ned told me they enjoyed meeting you and talking with you."

"Didn't you just get up?" I asked.

"I did. But one of them leaves me a report every night regarding what has gone on during the day. We need someone to look after our home during the day. They were highly recommended."

I nodded, my feelings of nervousness returning with a vengeance.

"Did you enjoy walking around? I know I'm biased, but I love my home," Collum said, and I could see that he was genuine.

"I did. I had a lot of time to think," I said.

His expression didn't change, but I could feel a shift in the atmosphere in the room.

"Did you come to any conclusions?"

I sighed. "I did. At least, I think I did."

Collum nodded, inviting me to continue.

"I really like you. I noticed that when you came in, and I was touching you, how much better I felt. And I realized that must be the effects of our connection," I said.

"It is."

"It is amazing, and I could have stayed close to you forever," I said, determined to be honest.

"Why are you over there, then?"

"Because I'm not ready to give up on my life. I spent the last year hiding from it, not living. And now, now that I'm finally awake again, now that I'm feeling more alive—you tell me that my life is already chosen for me, and that I must take one of two paths. Neither, I might add, allows me any agency." I hated saying this. I hated it.

I'd had the best sex I'd ever had with this man. Even now, the thought of being in bed with him, naked, was enough to give me goosebumps all over.

"What are you thinking?" Collum asked.

"You noticed that?" I smiled.

He nodded.

"I was thinking about how amazing last night was. But that's one night versus the rest of my life. And I'm not sure I'm ready to give up everything on the basis of one evening together."

His brows furrowed, the first sign that he was distressed by what I was saying. "There is more to it than the last twenty-four hours."

"Well, I don't know that. I've experienced essentially one day with you. And it's been an amazing day, a day unlike anything else I've ever experienced. I can see the benefits of being with someone you are perfectly matched with. But in order to experience life with you, I'd need to live here as a human, or become a vampire, right?"

He nodded.

"And since you're pretty opposed to making a vampire ever again, that really leaves me only one choice, doesn't it?"

Reluctantly, he nodded again.

"So really, there's only one option for me, isn't there?"

Even more slowly, he nodded a third time.

"That's not really enough for me, Collum," I stated with as much firmness as I could. I hated saying this. Hated it. But it had to be said. I'd spent the last year not being honest with myself, not facing reality, and if I wanted to move forward, that had to change. Starting now. Even as I would have rather avoided this conversation.

"That's... disappointing," Collum said, bringing me back to our conversation. "What can I do to ease this for you, make this more palatable?" His voice was steady, but I could hear the pain behind his words.

"I don't think there is anything you can do. You have been honest with me, and I appreciate it, more than you know. It's hard to be honest when that means you might not get what you want."

"I didn't even consider that you'd turn away from this," Collum said, sounding dazed.

"I get that. It was pretty clear most people and vampires don't turn away. But I have to be true to myself. I lost myself for the past year."

"If you feel being here, being with me, would be giving up life, you're making the right choice," Collum said, the sadness weighing down his words.

Oh, my God. I had to be the biggest, most elaborately prancing asshole on the planet. The. Biggest. "That's not what I meant. Does this, this— Bond? Does it ever go away?"

He shook his head.

"Then this is not it for us. But I don't think this is our time right now."

Collum opened his mouth and then shut it. He opened it again and clamped his lips together. "I have never forced anyone, human or vampire, to do something that collided with their own free will. I was, as you recall, made against my will. I do not regret it, but... I would not have chosen this way to start my second life." He sighed, crossing his arms and looking down at his feet. "You are welcome to stay here as long as you'd like, Isabeau."

"I need to leave tomorrow," I said. "Fergus or no Fergus. I have a schedule, and people who are expecting me."

"Right, yes, of course," he said. He looked up. "Would you be offended if I took my leave of you, then? I don't know if I can..." His voice trailed off.

"Of course not," I said quickly.

Moving with his vampire speed, he closed the distance between us and cradled me in his arms. His head ducked into my neck, and I felt that overwhelming sense of being close to him—my mate. I inhaled deeply, taking in the woodsy scent about him, and held him to me.

The tears started. I tried to hold them in, but I couldn't. Not when he held me like this, and I could feel his despair. I felt it myself.

I also knew I couldn't stay. I had to keep going. At least until the end of this task for my Gran. I'd left so much undone since the accident, and I couldn't do that again.

Not and stay myself.

"I will always be here for you, Isabeau." Collum stood up, taking my face in his hands and kissing me gently. "Always."

Then he was gone, the door to my room closing before I'd even gathered my wits from his kiss.

The room was silent. I was alone.

CHAPTER EIGHTEEN

Collum

I sped down to the library, where I knew Morag was waiting.

"Hey," she said as I entered the room. "What are—"

"Have you heard from the others?" I asked.

She nodded. "They sought him all last evening. They went to ground on the mainland, letting me know they planned to meet up and hunt before returning at dawn."

It was my turn to nod. "You should go hunt, as well."

"What happened?"

"Our guest will be leaving tomorrow," I said, and I couldn't conceal the ache the words brought.

"I'm so sorry, Collum," she said.

I waved a hand. "I am, too. But I cannot dwell, so I need something to do. You go and hunt, and I'll run the property."

Morag looked at me for a moment, considering. "You'll text if you need me back here?"

"Of course. I excel at delegating," I said, a tinge of bitterness creeping into my words.

She nodded, and ran from the room, leaving me alone with

my thoughts. Which was the last place I wanted to be. I paced the library, trying to make some sense of what in the god-awful hell had just happened.

I'd met her, met my mate, felt the bond, and bedded her. She was everything I'd hoped she would be, and more. I'd never expected to meet anyone else for me again, and to meet someone as amazing and strong as Isabeau? It was a gift.

But a gift she didn't want, a treasure that she didn't wish to share. I felt the liquid welling in my eyes. I let the blood fall, not caring that this was expending energy and nourishment.

I'd always knew that I'd end up alone. This confirmed it. The brief moments with her had given me hope, and that hope was gone.

The worst thing was I couldn't blame her. I understood why she'd made the decision she did. I could feel the conflict within her even as she made her stand for herself, for her own life. I understood. I didn't blame her.

But oh, how I wanted her to stay.

I allowed myself to cry for a bit more and then wiped the tears from my face. I went to the bathroom to wash my face, because if I was going on the hunt—for either MacDonald or a meal—I didn't need to have the blood on my face alerting anyone to my presence.

I zoomed into the kitchen where Constance was putting away the dishes from dinner.

"We're all going to be out this evening. I'm running a patrol, so if anything happens, text me?"

She nodded, smiling at me.

I ran from the kitchen before she could ask about Isabeau. She wanted to. I didn't have the strength to tell her that Isabeau was leaving, or that I completely understood why.

My heart beat still as I raced into the night, seeking the oblivion of the dark.

Four hours later, I stopped. I'd run the entire perimeter of my property. I knew MacDonald had been here, and recently. Within the last twenty-four hours, I'd bet. I couldn't be sure, but his scent was fresh.

He'd prowled my property lines, and he'd come in close to the house, only to retreat as far away as he could. He'd looked up at the house on the side where Isabeau's room was—which worried me. Why was he focused on her? She might not accept our bond, but I'd kill anyone or anything that tried to harm her. Without question.

I didn't want to go back to the house. I paced a little, running my hands through my hair. The glimpse of a different life had been so strong, so vivid—I'd thought of little else since last night. My rest during the day today had been restless, as images of Isabeau moved through my dreams.

I was debating which way to go when I was knocked over from behind.

Then everything went dark.

When I opened my eyes, it was still night. My fangs were extended, and I could feel the rush of adrenaline that was present right before a battle. So I was still outside, and I'd guess it was the same evening I'd been attacked from behind since I hadn't turned to dust. I was still in the woods.

A rustle of footsteps, the smallest of movement of a shoe upon grass. I sprang to my feet and crouched low and spun around, seeking him.

It was MacDonald. The area around me was redolent with the scent I'd been smelling. It had to be him.

"Where are you?" I whispered.

FOREVER BLOOD

"I'm everywhere, Collum MacLean." His voice was quiet, rich with the accent of a Highlander. And not one from recent times. I recalled what I'd heard about him – he was older than me. It took me back to my village, to the waiting on the boat, and then on the beach—right before I was made.

"Why are you here, MacDonald?" I kept my own voice quiet. "You are in violation of the rules of this island. My coven will not stand for it."

"I am not here to hunt," he said.

"Then why are you here?"

Silence, and then, "To rectify my mistakes."

A ringing blow to my skull.

"To find redemption." His voice lowered, almost a hiss.

A hit to the other side of my skull.

He was fast, very fast. I'd not even seen him coming. Yeah, he was older than I was.

"I cannot give you that," I said, wanting him to talk. He would be easier to find.

"Yes, you can. You are one of the last. So many did not survive," MacDonald said.

"What are you talking about?"

"My children," he said. "You are one of my oldest children. You were not meant to be made, Collum MacLean. You were supposed to die on that beach, and it was only because another man came upon me feeding and struck me with an axe that any of my blood transferred to you."

"What?" I asked.

"You should have died five hundred years ago. You were a mistake. And you are one that I must rectify."

"Why?" I'd pinpointed where his voice was coming from. He was just beyond a small grove of trees, clustered together and forming a barrier. I'd need to have him talking, keep him distracted.

At least, I hoped that's what would happen. My luck wasn't

115

looking all that great today. Again. Lady Luck really hated me lately.

"I made a vampire without permission. I've dealt with him." His voice held great satisfaction. " I am able to present myself to the Council in Edinburgh; show them I did not mean to break the law. But you—if they were to know of you, my return would be lost to me forever."

"This is all so you can be around your kind again?" My voice rose in disbelief.

"Of course. What else would it be?"

"You left me to die! I spent years trying to figure out how to live this new life! How many humans died because you left me alone, with no guidance, no aid, no teachings?"

"Humans die. You were human once—I was not. I was born vampire, and I was always careful with those I chose to make. You, Collum MacLean, were nothing more than a mistake. You've been a fairly resourceful mistake, I'll admit. I never expected you to last as long as you did. However, that time is over."

A slight whisper of fabric against leaves, and then all was silent.

The time for speaking was over.

Another whisper of movement and I felt something slash my arm. I whirled at the impact, nearly falling to the ground, but catching myself, I leapt at the form passing me. I caught the tail end of his jacket. Hooking my hand, I yanked him to me for all I was worth.

He hit me, a wall of solid muscle and sinew. We went down, and at that point, there was nothing but the fight in front of me.

He rolled to the right, springing to his hands and feet, and launched himself at me.

I fell backward with a thud and got my arms up to wrap my fingers around his throat.

Despite the pressure of my hands, he pressed into me, his head going lower than my chin.

I wondered what the hell he was doing. I couldn't strangle him, as we could go without air for longer than humans, but I could break his neck. If I got the right angle.

I heard the snap of his fangs near my neck and the reality of the situation hit me.

He was trying to bite me, and he planned to drain me. So that I would not be around to be a witness to his crime.

For he told the truth. This was my sire, my maker. I could feel it, the pull. And he was trying to kill me.

No! I shouted inside my head. *No!* He'd already taken so much from me. I'd already had to live with the consequences of his actions. I would not continue to do so. After five hundred years of trying to live with what had been done to me, I would not die to make his continued existence easier!

"No!" I grunted, shoving him off me. The movement startled him, but he recovered quickly. He landed on his feet.

"It's no use. You can't defeat me," MacDonald said, a smug tone in his voice. "Give up now, MacLean, and I'll do it quick. I'll even leave that spicy redhead and the rest of your coven alone."

Listening to his words, it was as if a red curtain had been drawn across my line of vision. This smug, smarmy, piece of shit wanker. He wasn't getting my coven, or my Isabeau. She was mine, just like the rest of my coven, and even if I didn't make it, I was taking him with me.

I lunged for his legs, my nails elongating and my fangs out. Catching hold of his right leg, I raked at it with my hands and bit into the leg above the knee. He howled and kicked, shaking me off.

He was strong.

But I had greater reason to kill him.

He fought only for himself.

I fought for all those I loved.

As I landed on my back from where he'd thrown me, MacDonald fell upon me, and bit at my collar bone. I cried out and punched him in the face.

He rolled to the side, clutching his nose. "It will not be slow, MacLean," he said with menace.

I didn't respond, but launched myself at him again, aiming to bite at his neck. His vision was obscured by the hand still clutching his nose, and I got purchase and bit into the juncture where his neck met his torso.

His blood made my head swim. I sucked furiously, knowing that I didn't have time. It would give me strength—as I finished the thought, he tossed me from him with a roar and with such violence that my fangs ached. Before I could move, MacDonald landed on me, and I felt him bite at my neck. He was not careful, and he tore at my skin.

He was so fast. My strength began to fade as he fed from me. My hands fell to either side. I was so tired. There was something scratching at my hand and my head rolled to the right of me to see my hand resting atop a stick.

What was it about a stick that was important, I wondered? I could feel the pain at my neck, but it was beginning to fade, to feel like something happening at a distance. Why was a stick important? It seemed that I should remember something.

A stick.

My fingers scrabbled to get the stick, and with an effort, I raised my hand. The man on top of me was feeding from me, noisy and harsh, and he didn't see my arm moving. I raised my left arm, bringing my hands together to clasp the stick.

All I needed was to stake him, and he would let go. Leave me be. Let me rest.

The pain in my neck grew stronger, and I arched up, trying to get away.

I brought my hands down, wanting nothing more than to

curl into a ball, to make the pain go away. I just had to get this thing off me. It was in my way.

The dreadful ache at my neck disappeared.

"What have you done?" I heard someone shouting. "What have you done?"

The shouting ended abruptly. I didn't know why, but the pain in my neck had stopped. That was good. I wished that Isabeau was with me. Isabeau with the beautiful red hair, the laughing mouth, the silky white arms and legs. "I'm sorry, Isabeau," I murmured.

With the pain gone, I could close my eyes. I was so tired.

"I'm sorry," I said once more. "Sorry."

Then the night went dark. I was safe, and I could close my eyes.

CHAPTER NINETEEN

ISABEAU

I sat up in bed. Someone had screamed. "Collum?" I asked.

There was no answer. But I'd heard the scream, and I could feel fear coursing through me.

"Collum?" I said again, louder this time.

The house gave no response.

I got out of bed, and pulled on my shoes, heading for Collum's room next door. I knocked, and when there was no answer from within, I opened the door.

Normally, I would have liked to snoop all over the place, but the sense of urgency was growing. "Collum?" I called out.

No answer.

I ran down the hallway, and then down the stairs. Into the library. No one was there. I checked in the dining room, a room that looked like a study, and then headed for the kitchen.

Constance was in, a single light from the stove illuminating her kind face as she put the kettle on the burner. She turned as I raced in. "Isabeau! Is everything all right?"

"I don't know. I woke up when I heard a scream."

"I didn't hear anything." Her face creased in worry.

"Where are the other vampires?" I asked.

"Morag went hunting, and the others are still on the mainland," she said, looking even more worried. "I'll go get Ned."

"Did you see Collum tonight?"

She shook her head. "No. Only Morag, who told me Collum was running the perimeter, and she was heading over to the mainland."

Shit.

I ran past her and out the back door.

"Where are you going? Isabeau, it's not safe!" I heard her yell.

No, it wasn't safe. Collum was in danger. I had no idea how I knew, but I knew. I had to find him. Nothing else mattered.

"Where are you?" I muttered. Then I stopped. It wouldn't do me, or Collum, any good to run around like a chicken, and hope I'd stumble over him. That wasn't going to work.

We were mates, he'd said. And I'd felt the connection when we were close. There was something there I'd never felt with anyone before.

Okay. Then I needed to use it. I stopped, taking a couple of deep breaths, and closed my eyes. The noises of the woods around the house were different at night. There was something menacing in them—but I had to find Collum.

No matter what.

I didn't know how I knew, but I knew. I had to find him.

"Where are you?" I asked quietly, trying to calm my racing heart and my rattled nerves. "Let me find you, Collum."

There was no answer from the surrounding trees. But— I turned slightly to my left. There was something. Not a voice, but more like I was being pulled.

"Okay," I said. It was better than nothing.

I followed the pull. As I went deeper into the woods, my palms were sweaty, and I could feel the beads of moisture running down my back even though it was cool tonight. Something was wrong. Collum was hurt, or in trouble. Whatever was going on with him was making me sweat—literally.

And I was going the right way. I had no idea how I knew that, but I did.

After what seemed like a marathon's distance, I came to a clearing. There was something there, something moving...

"Collum!" I screamed, running for the heap in the center of the small clearing. "Collum!"

It was too late when I realized this might not be Collum at all. I tried to put the brakes on, but that didn't work, and I tripped, and fell over whatever the heap was.

My first instincts had been right. The heap was Collum, and he was in a bad way. A really bad way.

"Collum? What in the hell happened?"

He stirred, mumbling. He was covered in blood and some kind of sticky dirt. It was gross. I pulled at his shoulder and rolled him onto his back. Leaning down, I spoke quietly. "Collum? What happened? What do I need to do?"

He didn't stir, didn't make a sound. And then his eyes flew open so fast I jumped back. "Isabeau?" His voice was raspy, tired.

"I'm here. What happened?"

"Mac—MacDonald," he whispered. "Gone now."

"Did you kill him?" I asked, slipping an arm beneath his shoulders and bringing him into my lap.

"Think so," he said so low that I almost didn't hear it. "Safe. You're... safe." His eyes closed then, and he sighed, obviously tired.

"Dying," he said, his eyes still closed.

"What? He's still around? And dying?" I felt panic rise in my throat, a sour taste that made me think I might throw up.

"No. Me. Dying," he rasped.

"What? No!" I clutched him to me, tears springing to my eyes. "You can't die! No, no, Collum, you can't die!"

"Sorry," he whispered. "Safe. All safe." I felt him sag against me, giving new meaning to the phrase 'dead weight.'

"No, you can't go," I cried, tears falling down my face and onto his. "No!"

He murmured something but I couldn't hear it.

In my head, I heard him telling me about Sarah. How he'd drained her, and then given her his blood, and taken her to bed with him, waiting for her to wake up.

He couldn't die. I was ready to leave when I went to bed tonight, but now, covered in his blood and whatever dirt and gunk he'd been rolling in, I knew that I couldn't let him die.

Not when I could help him. I couldn't lose him, too. Not again.

"You need to eat," I said. I put my hand near his mouth. I'd seen it in a movie, so who knew how accurate it would be? But it would get the blood to him fast, and that was the point.

I'd had no intentions of letting him bite me again mere hours before, but now, there was nothing else in the world that I wanted.

"Eat," I said, putting my wrist on his mouth. "You need to eat."

Collum turned his head, and I pulled it back to where I could see it. His eyes were closed, and he was pale even in the moonlight. It might be my imagination, but he looked paler than normal.

Shit shit shit.

I didn't know what to do. Looking down at Collum, his mouth parted slightly, and I saw the glimmer of his fang.

Fangs!

I lifted up his lip and put my wrist to his fang. Taking a breath, I scraped my wrist hard along his fang, and I stifled a scream as the skin broke.

I was not at all prepared for him.

He latched on to my wrist, biting deeper. I felt him drink

from me, and I could actually feel the blood leaving me. He continued to drink, and... wow. I was tired. I tugged at my hand, wanting to take my wrist back and lie down. But he was holding onto me too tightly, and it was too much effort to fight with him. I lay my head on his chest and let him keep my hand. I'd just close my eyes for a minute.

The next thing I knew was I was being shaken, and someone was yelling. God, he was loud. I was too tired to deal with it right now. "Leave me alone," I said.

Whoever it was, he wasn't listening. Just like a man, I thought. Too busy talking to listen. Well, he wouldn't listen to me, so no need to try. I sighed and tried to tune him out. Maybe he'd shut up.

His voice was like nails on a chalkboard, aggravating me when all I wanted was to go to sleep. I took a breath, which was harder than I thought it should be. I'd just... I'd just...

CHAPTER TWENTY

Collum

I couldn't believe her. I could not believe her. She'd given herself up for me. When I'd felt the drop of blood in my mouth, I felt there might be a chance. When the blood was offered up, I drank, uncaring of the source. When sense returned, and I'd seen who was collapsed across my chest, I'd sprang up.

No! No! I held her to me, listening for her heartbeat. My own heart hadn't beat once since I'd collapsed. I knew that MacDonald was gone. There was ash all over and around me, and I was still alive. If my memory was correct, I'd staked him. I struggled to believe it, but the ash and my continued existence would suggest it was as my hazy memory recalled.

None of that mattered right now. What mattered was saving Isabeau.

I felt another vampire approaching. I rose to a crouch, hovering over her and seeking the direction the vampire was coming from.

It was Talbot and Charlotte.

"Collum! Where is the danger?" Talbot asked.

I relaxed my stance. "He's all over the clearing," I said. "Will you keep watch? I didn't sense anyone else, but I need to heal her."

"She is near death," Charlotte said, leaning over Isabeau. "There is not much time, Collum, if you plan to—"

"I know!" I snapped, feeling my fangs descend. This was my mate. I knew what needed to be done.

But she'd just told me she didn't want to be a vampire. She was planning to leave. She also hadn't planned to let me bite her again—and when it came to it, she gave me what I needed so that I wouldn't die.

Could I do any less? There was only one thing I could do. If Isabeau wasn't happy with my choice, I'd do what I could to give her a life she was happy with—and I would guess that would not include me.

If it kept her alive, I would do it.

I bit at my wrist and offered it to her pale lips. She was still alive, but barely.

Her mouth parted, the drops of blood staining her lips. They moved, and her tongue darted out, tasting the blood. Her hand slowly rose and pulled my wrist to her mouth. She drank, slowly at first, and then with increasing strength, although it was not the strength of a healthy woman.

Her hand dropped and her head lolled to the side.

"It is done," Charlotte said. "We need to bring her inside and get her settled."

"She'll stay with me," I said, scooping her up into my arms.

The three of us moved back to the house, slower than normal because I didn't want to jostle her. I knew that the blood from me was healing her, changing her—and nothing I did now would matter, but I wasn't going to be anything other than gentle with Isabeau.

My heart thumped once, and then again. It meant she was still alive and still fighting.

"Fight, my love. Fight," I whispered to her. "Fight for us. Fight for you."

She didn't move. She was barely breathing.

But she was healing. The next step was to see if her body would accept my blood and make the change from human to a vampire.

I didn't want to think about it, but I could think of nothing else. I brought Isabeau to my room and settled her into the bed I'd built under my bed. It was a box—the kind you sometimes saw in the news—where I could sleep in comfort and darkness. It hid beneath the traditional seventeenth century tall bed.

I tucked her in and closed the lid on the box, lowering the faux bed over top it. I wasn't ready to sleep yet, even if that was where she needed to be.

"Where is everyone else?" I asked Talbot.

"They are on their way home. None of us found MacDonald, but you did. What happened?"

"I was..." I stopped. How to tell them all that happened? Honestly, if not in great detail. "I told Isabeau the truth. About me, about our bond. She was not... impressed." I felt myself frown as I remembered that conversation. It still ached.

Talbot laughed. "I was not expecting to hear that! She's got some spirit."

"She does, indeed." I looked back at the bed. "I hope it will carry her through."

"It will. This may not be what you or she planned, but this will work," Talbot said.

I heard doors opening below as the rest of my coven—hopefully the rest of them—returned home. First Lyall and Clara, who came in holding hands. They always did. I liked seeing it. It gave me hope.

Then Margaret and Devon, and Angus and Kyla. Morag was the last one in. They all looked at me, and I could see and feel the worry for me, for Isabeau.

"Did she want to become one of us?" Clara asked.

I shook my head. "She said she'd just learned how to live again and wasn't willing to give that up right now."

Talbot shook his head. "She may feel differently once she wakes."

"If—" I began.

"No!" Charlotte held up a hand to me. "No. What happened to you previously was an aberration. More vampires are made than not. This will be fine, Collum."

"Did you find the human who was with MacDonald?" I asked, not wanting to dwell on it. Hearing them talk about it made all my concern go right into overdrive.

Margaret said, "We did. We were insistent he tell us what he knew, despite his reluctance." She made a face.

I burst out laughing despite the strain of everything else tonight. "Is he still alive, Margaret? I've seen your insistence."

Devon smiled. "She was restrained. He's a regular piece of shit, but he's still walking around, waiting to inflict pain on someone else."

"I'm glad," I said. "We don't need dead humans."

"Tell us about MacDonald," Morag said. "I am so sorry I left you, Collum." Her eyes were wide, and I thought she might cry. "Did he nearly drain you?"

"He did. I was not in the here and now when Isabeau found me."

"How did she find you?" Lyall asked.

I shrugged. "I don't know. We didn't have a chance to talk."

"What do you remember?"

"I'm fairly certain I staked MacDonald. I had the ash all over me," I said.

A shudder passed through the group. That was a surefire way to kill us, and no one liked to think of it. Although I had to admit I wasn't feeling any guilt over MacDonald.

"Before he died, he told me why he was hunting me."

"Why?" Angus spoke for everyone.

"He was my sire," I said.

"What?" Morag said. "That makes no sense."

"No, it didn't, but he was happy to explain. The record you found that he'd been banished for making a vampire without permission?"

I nodded, impatient to hear it all.

"That wasn't the only vampire he made. He made me by accident. He was interrupted while feeding on me, and someone on the beach hit him with an axe. He was quite happy to inform me I would have never had his blood otherwise."

Kyla, the youngest of us, rolled her eyes. "God, some of you old-timers are such pretentious douchebags."

Morag and Devon laughed.

"I'd think this was probably his nature no matter how old he was," I said. "Anyway, he was cleaning up the evidence. He's been on the run since then— Well, he had," I amended, remembering with vicious pleasure that Fergus MacDonald was now a thing of the past.

"So he's a jackass to boot," Kyla said. "Good riddance."

I smiled at her. She was a good match for Angus. He was one of the old timers she complained about, but once he'd met her, there was no one else for either of them.

"I don't think we need to worry about any other vampires coming to avenge him," Morag said. "It sounds as though he operated in secret."

"We'll need to let the council in Edinburgh know," Margaret said. She was cross.

The council were also what Kyla would call pretentious douchebags.

"You should do it," Charlotte said to Margaret. "Not one of them can hold a candle to you."

Margaret made a noise of derision, but I could feel her pleasure at Charlotte's words.

"Let's get through tonight," Margaret said. "Collum, go and clean up, and be with Isabeau."

The rest of the coven nodded at her words.

"We'll lock up, Dad," Clara teased me.

"Thank you," I said.

"Shout at me if you need us," Lyall told me.

I nodded.

They filed out of my room and I raced through a shower. When I got out, I saw that someone had left bags of blood on the bed. That was good. I'd been so concerned over everything else that I forgot she'd be hungry as hell. I'd need to give her blood immediately and hope she didn't bite me.

When I opened up my sleeping box, Isabeau was where I'd left her.

A thought hit me. My heart had not beaten since I'd brought her back to the house. What did that mean? I could feel the panic hit me like an axe over the head.

Climbing into bed, I pulled the lid and bed down over top us.

I asked Sarah to look down on Isabeau. I could think of no one better to pray to. Sarah would have understood.

While I closed my eyes, I did not sleep. At the dawning, when I felt sleepy, I could feel the worry for Isabeau keep me from a true rest.

Only twelve more hours, thirty-seven minutes, and fourteen seconds until we'd be at night once more.

Please, I thought. *Please let her wake.*

CHAPTER TWENTY-ONE

ISABEAU

When I woke, I grabbed at my throat. It burned. "Wa—" I said and then I choked, and coughed, and sneezed.

What the hell was happening here? I sat up and hit my head. "Ow!" I yelled.

Which hurt my throat, and made me clutch at it again, as though massaging would ease the aching burn.

"Isabeau, you're hungry," a male voice—Collum—said.

Something was put to my lips, something that smelled delicious and metallic and I drank, greedily, gulping.

The burn eased. I drank until the pouch I held ran dry and shoved it away. "More," I croaked.

Another pouch came in front of me. It was so weird to be lying here in the dark, drinking metallic water out of a pouch. I could hear the rustling as I moved on the bed. I was on a bed, it was just a bed inside of something with a lid, which had connotations I didn't really want to consider.

Well, I'd consider them in a moment. After I had more to drink. A third and fourth pouch were offered to me, and I drank them both. Finishing the fourth, I stopped and took a breath.

Everything smelled different. I could taste the smells. I was in a box—I could smell and taste the surrounding wood.

And the person with me was Collum. I could smell him. He smelled wonderful. After I addressed this dry throat thing, I'd have to get closer to him and his wonderful smell.

"How are you?" His voice seemed loud in the small space.

I could hear outside of wherever it was we were as well. There were people moving around, although they were... different.

What the hell?

"What is going on?" I asked carefully, taking my time. My throat didn't burn, but the desire for more was there. Like when you eat, and you're still hungry. And there's no food around.

"Do you need more?"

"Yes," I said. Another pouch appeared in front of me, and I drank it. "I am so thirsty," I said. At least I wasn't croaking. I felt like I should be, but I sounded almost like myself.

"You're not thirsty. You're hungry," he said.

Whatever, I thought.

"No, you are. When you are feeling steadier, we'll get up and we need to speak."

"I'd like to get up now," I said. I didn't mind the darkness, or the small space. It felt cozy, and more importantly, safe. That was something I hadn't felt for some time. Not since I'd looked behind me and seen a wall of white and I couldn't find my friends.

My God. It had been that long.

The lid over the bed lifted, and I could see that Collum's room was lit by low light, and it was night. I sat up and nearly fell over because I moved so fast. I was out of the weird box-under-the-bed as fast as I could. What the hell was this? A sex slave set up? That was the kind of people who slept in boxes under the bed. Good thing I was moving so fast.

Moving so fast.

Wait a minute. One. Damn. Minute.

There was only one person I'd seen move fast like this. I looked at Collum. He watched me carefully—almost too carefully. I whirled around to look at Collum, who'd also gotten out of the bed cave and was lowering what looked like a normal bed over it. I forced myself to breathe. He wasn't a trafficker—he sure wasn't normal. I remembered the conversation where he explained the whole vampire thing. But I didn't get someone who traded in human suffering.

Well, not really. Vampire, remember?

This was getting me nowhere. If I let my mind keep going like this, I was going to go insane in approximately ten minutes.

He was a vampire. They needed to sleep in darkness. It wasn't a cave to hide women. *Breathe,* I told myself. *Breathe.*

"What happened?" I asked. This seemed like the safest place to start.

He sighed. "What do you remember, Isabeau?"

I thought about it. What did I want to know first? "I ran out to look for you. And it was weird—" I looked over at him. "It was like, following a radar or something. I don't know how I found you. But I did. And you were dying!" I reached over to touch him. He wasn't as cool to the touch as he'd been when we were naked together. Now he felt... normal. Not a trafficker or cold or anything. "But obviously you didn't."

He shook his head. "No, I survived. Do you remember anything else?"

"I made you take some blood from my wrist, and then I remember wanting to go to sleep. That's all I remember," I said slowly, trying to make sense of the flashes of people talking over me.

"You were near death."

"You drank that much from me?" I pulled away.

"I didn't mean to, but I was dying, and I... I didn't have as much control as I usually do. I stopped myself."

"Thank you?" I asked, trying to keep the sarcasm out of my voice. "Not exactly a great date, Collum."

He smiled. For the first time, I noticed the sadness that tinged his smile. How had I not seen that before?

"No, you didn't get to see me at my best."

"Did you kill Fergus?" I asked, afraid of the answer. I couldn't even believe I was asking this.

"I did, although the details are a little hazy. He was trying to drain me." His hand crept up to his neck.

"Did he bite you?"

He nodded. "Right here," he touched the base of his neck.

"No way. There's no wound there!"

"We heal quickly."

"I guess so. Okay, so he wanted to drain you. Why?"

"He was my sire by accident. He wasn't supposed to make me, and he was cleaning up his mistake," Collum said quietly. "But do you want to talk about that, or do you want to talk about you?"

"What's wrong with me?" I asked. "I feel great, greater than great." I stopped. "Starving, thirsty, but great. Maybe we do need to talk about me. Why do I feel great? Didn't you nearly kill me?"

He winced. "I did. So... I healed you."

"How?" I asked. This one, I knew I didn't want to know the answer, but I asked anyway.

"I gave you my blood."

Oh. "Um, well. I wasn't expecting that, but if it saved me, thank you. Are there magic powers that go along with this?"

"What do you mean?" he asked.

"I've seen all the vampire shows," I said crossly. "I get super strength, or I can fly, or see through walls—something!"

"We don't fly. No x-ray vision. We are strong, and very fast."

Fast. I'd moved fast. Oh. Oh, no. Oh, shit. "Collum, am I..." I asked in a whisper as the realization hit me.

"I turned you so that you would not die, Isabeau."

I looked at him, trying to comprehend. Then I took a deep breath and found that I could taste the air. I could—holy shit. I could *taste* the fear coming from Collum. He really, really didn't want to tell me.

"You turned me?" I whispered. I could feel the rage building in me. He knew I didn't want this.

"You would have died if I had not."

"I—" I stopped. I had told him I wasn't ready to give up my life so easily—but when it came down to it, I'd given up my life without a thought to feed him, to heal him.

Maybe the lady protests a little too much? Weird bed aside.

I shoved that away. I didn't want to be mad at myself. I wanted to be mad at Collum, the proper place for anger and stomping and witty sarcastic barbs.

But I was the one who'd used his fang to cut my wrist so he could eat. So he wouldn't die. I'd done what I needed to do for him. I could see him still, lying on the ground, the blood seeping from him, black and glistening. It was the second most horrible thing I'd ever seen. And this time, I did what I could. To save someone I cared for.

Just like he'd done for me.

I didn't think I was going to get to stomp around and yell tonight. I mean, I couldn't but why? For all my denial, when a choice was required, I'd chosen him. He'd done the same.

Bond, the mate thing—whatever. We'd chosen one another.

"Isabeau? Are you unwell?"

I looked at him. "Why?"

"You've been silent for the past fifteen minutes."

"I was thinking. Isn't this supposed to be some big thing? Like, I can be normal or go crazy or something?" I asked.

Collum laughed, and there was a different note in his laugh, one I hadn't heard before. "No, you've done the hard part, the change. The question is always whether you'll survive. Now you get to live as a vampire."

"I need to unpick a lot of things, Collum," I said. I might have come back from the dead, but the life I'd had as a human was still there.

"We'll help you with that."

"But my family! My friends!"

"You've fallen for a guy who is allergic to sunlight," he said.

I looked at him and then burst out laughing. "Are you kidding me?"

"I've known a number of vampires who used it to great success," he said, grinning.

"That is almost the craziest thing I've ever heard," I said. "Is that even a thing?"

"It is. Look it up. I have to ask you, though. What changed your mind?" Collum asked.

"Well, that went sideways quick," I said. "What do you mean?"

"You told me two nights ago that you were leaving, that you didn't want to see what the mating bond could offer. That you didn't want to be turned." His eyes were serious, and all the laughter was gone.

"I didn't want to die," I said, stressing the 'die' bit. "I had to die to be with you. Oh, I know you said there were choices." I waved a hand. "But there was really only one choice. And I didn't want to make it, and I didn't want to have someone, or something, make it for me."

"I made it for you," Collum replied.

"No, you didn't. I made it. When I came looking for you, and I made you feed from me—I made my choice. I didn't know it at the time. I didn't even know it until about five minutes ago. But I made it. When I thought you were going to die, I didn't even hesitate, even though I know what you eat, and that you've killed people." I sighed. "And while I really wanted to scream and yell at you, I realized that you'd made the same choice— that when you thought I was going to die, you did what you could to keep me alive, even if this doesn't really count."

He looked at me, and then looked away, then looked at me once more. "You're only twenty-two, and you sorted that out in the space of time from when you woke up?"

I nodded smugly. "Women are like that. Modern women even more so."

He laughed again.

"Hey, don't think this conversation is over. We have a lot more to discuss," I said, giving him my best evil eye. "But there are other things I'd rather do than tell you what you've done wrong."

"What do you want to do?"

"I want to go outside and get to know the new me. Have something more to eat."

He stood, holding my hand and pulling me to my feet. "Let's go see the new world," he said with a smile.

CHAPTER TWENTY-TWO

Collum

I watched Isabeau run ahead of me. I scouted for any danger, any people, any anything that might harm her. When new vampires first went outside, sometimes the enhanced awareness of everything was enough to send one screaming into madness. It was just so much to process. As a new vampire, one was often unaware of lurking dangers.

Hence why a sire stayed close to those they made.

I thought of my sire, now ash in the forest. He'd left me, and from what he said, he didn't feel bad about it. I'd been lucky to survive.

All these years of having no one who shared my blood—I'd been strong enough to survive. Not only survive, but to thrive.

I'd lost my first mate, but it allowed me to change my path, and create a life for myself that was more to my liking. I'd gathered like-minded vampires and created a coven. We were together not because blood bound us, but because we chose to be.

But now, now... I also had the ties of blood. I could sense

what Isabeau was feeling, although it was muted. Not only was she made by me, she was my mate.

The level of contentment and happiness was unimaginable. This was what I'd been missing.

I heard Isabeau laugh, and her laughter made me smile.

There was still much to do. To manage her family, and her life before this. I hadn't mentioned it, but in addition to the sun allergy, there would be some glamour on our part. That way, her parents and family wouldn't make a fuss. We'd lived quietly here for two hundred years. No need to upset all that.

I felt a singing in my blood; an exhilaration I hadn't felt in decades. The night smelled sweeter, and more enticing. Once Isabeau decided she was done, we'd go home. Together.

She was not only my mate, and part of my coven, she was my blood, and we'd be bound by that blood tie forever.

Forever blood, I thought. Forever.

With a grin, I raced to catch up with her. We had forever.

Love the Clan MacLean?
Read on for an excerpt from the next book from my collaboration
with the Midnight Coven, Immortal Darkness.

VAMPIRE MATES

Preview of Immortal Darkness
From the Vampire Mates series

Morag

I watched my coven mates, arms crossed over my chest. All of them were in full lovey dovey mode. Even Collum, the head of our clan. He'd recently found Isabeau, and while it hadn't been planned, he'd turned her. Now they were together, and while I was happy for him, a small part of my heart ached for me. I wouldn't admit it to anyone else, but there was a small ache.

I'd been vampire for over one hundred years. In all that time, I'd never found anyone who made my quieted heart beat once more. Fifty years ago, I'd spent time prowling the city streets, looking for someone who would ring my bell, give me a heartbeat, show me the way.

It hadn't happened.

So now, I just found men to bed. It was satisfying, and there were no strings. In fact, I decided that with all the love in the air, it would be a great time for me to take a weekend for myself and leave the rest of my coven to manage things here.

Collum felt my change of mood. He'd always been the one who had been most attuned to me. Even after mating with Isabeau, he was still the first one to sense my thoughts.

"What is it, Morag?" he asked.

"I think I'm taking a weekend off. Not like any of you plan to leave the house. And with all ten of you here, there is no one foolish enough to take you on," I grinned.

Collum laughed, something that he did now that Isabeau had come into his life. I liked the change in him, and I liked her. Her family had come to visit, and everyone but Collum and I had left. We presented ourselves as brother and sister, both deathly allergic to the sun.

"Good thing you live in Scotland," Isabeau's grandmother had said.

Once Isabeau told them she was hand fast with Collum, and no desire to leave, her grandmother sighed and told Collum and me to call her Gran. I couldn't remember my real grandmother, and the feeling of her patting my arm brought a warmth over me I hadn't expected.

So Isabeau was a good addition to our clan.

But that still left me, all on my own.

Clara nodded at me, understanding, as did Kyla. No one else made any comment, and later that night, after a bracing run in the woods, I made plans to go into Edinburgh. There was enough diversity there I'd be able to find someone to spend the night with and feed. All while flying under the radar.

I raced into Edinburgh on Thursday evening, making for the club district. I had some time before dawning and I was restless and wanted to dance and maybe feed before I went to ground for the day. I preferred Old Town and Candlemaker Row for student pubs. Tonight it was Cabaret Voltaire. It was small, dark, and old. Perfect for hunting for sex, or food, or both.

The bouncers knew me, so I breezed through the front, not waiting in line. The vibe tonight was delicious. There was an air of searching, of wanting—my favorite kinds of nights. I went straight to the bar and got a glass of red wine. I wouldn't drink it, but these evenings went better if I had a glass of something in my hand. While I waited on my drink, I surveyed the bar. Lots of men here. The women would come later.

Most were young, and out with their friends, having a good time. That wasn't what I wanted tonight. I looked around, not seeing anyone who—wait. I stared at the entrance. The hair on the back of my neck stood on end.

The light from the outside of the doorway framed a man. Tall, dark, emanating danger.

"Yes, please," I purred, pushing myself off the bar.

This has been an amazing project with the authors of the Midnight Coven. The vampires are so much fun to write, and the other authors are fantastic to work with.

We have a Facebook group where you can keep up with all the things we're doing (read on for an excerpt from our next project!). And don't miss out on any of the novellas in the Vampires Brides series!

Forever Claimed by Kim Loraine
Forever Magnolia by Dyan Chick
Forever Blood by Lisa Manifold
Forever Kept by Patricia D. Eddy
Forever Still by Corinne O'Flynn
Forever Desired by Ariel Marie
Forever Onyx by Alice K. Wayne
Forever Chosen by K.L. Bone
Forever Immortal by Amelia Hutchins
Forever Taboo by Nichole Chase
Forever Bound by Karpov Kinrade

ABOUT THE AUTHOR

Lisa Manifold is a *USA Today* Bestselling Author of fantasy, paranormal, and romance stories. She moved to Colorado as an adult and has no plans of living anywhere else. She is a consummate reader, often running late because "Just one more page!" She is a fan of all things Con, and has an entire room devoted to the costumes created for Cons.

Lisa is the author of many flavors of paranormal series, including The Realm, Djinn Everlasting, Dragon Thief, The Aumahnee Prophecy, Tales from the Veil, Sisters of the Curse, the books from The Midnight Coven collective, and the upcoming Deadwood Sisters and The Mostly Open Paranormal Investigative Agency.

She lives as close to the mountains as possible with her husband, children, and four red rescue dogs.

Stay in touch:
Sign up for my Newsletter and never miss a thing!
Website: www.lisamanifold.com
Or one of the links below.

ALSO BY LISA MANIFOLD

Vampire Brides

(with The Midnight Coven)

Forever Blood

Deadwood Sisters

Hellborn: The Unlucky Book 1 (June 2019)

Dragon Thief

Dragon Lost

Dragon Found

The Realm Series

Heart of the Goblin King

To Wed the Goblin King

Realms of the Goblin King

Rise of the Dragon King

The Companion Tales, Volume I

The Companion Tales, Volume II

The Aumahnee Prophecy

with Corinne O'Flynn

Eamonn's Tale

Marigold's Tale

Watchers of the Veil

Defenders of the Realm

Tales From The Veil

with Corinne O'Flynn

The Portal Keepers

The Gimcrackers

Djinn Everlasting

Three Wishes

Forgotten Wishes

Hidden Wishes

Sisters of the Curse

Thea's Tale

One Night at the Ball

Casimir's Journey

Do you like being in the loop? Sign up for Lisa's newsletter! Shenanigans, book recs, and the latest news abound!